CONGREGATION OF THE DEAD

Solomon Islands, 1942: On Guadalcanal the Americans are fighting the bloodiest battle of the Pacific campaign. Behind the Japanese lines, a handful of British and Australian coastwatchers, aided by loyal Solomon Islanders, strive desperately to avoid capture and certain death, yet at the same time endeavour to keep the Americans informed of enemy movements. But they also conduct an unrelenting private war against each other . . .

GRAEME KENT

CONGREGATION OF THE DEAD

Complete and Unabridged

LINFORD
Leicester

First published in Great Britain in 1983 by
Robert Hale Limited
London

First Linford Edition
published 2001
by arrangement with
Robert Hale Limited
London

British Library CIP Data

Kent, Graeme
Congregation of the dead.—Large print ed.—
Linford mystery library
1. Detective and mystery stories
2. Large type books
I. Title
823.9'14 [F]

ISBN 0–7089–5987–3

Published by
F. A. Thorpe (Publishing)
Anstey, Leicestershire

Set by Words & Graphics Ltd.
Anstey, Leicestershire
Printed and bound in Great Britain by
T. J. International Ltd., Padstow, Cornwall

This book is printed on acid-free paper

Author's Note

The exploits of the coastwatchers of the Solomon Islands and New Guinea during the Second World War are perhaps not as widely known as they should be, but as Admiral Halsey said: 'The coastwatchers saved Guadalcanal. And Guadalcanal saved the Pacific.'

The names of some of these men are mentioned in this book, as are those of such famous personages as General Vandegrift and Admiral Halsey. But although the background is as genuine as reasearch can make it, all the main characters in this novel are fictional and bear no resemblance to anyone living or dead. I have created an entirely new district of the Solomon Islands. Renbanga and its neighbouring islands will be found on no map, just as the men and women who occupy them never existed.

The man that wandereth out of the way of understanding shall remain in the congregation of the dead.

Proverbs 21:16

1

He had been watching the airstrip since first light and his arms were aching with the strain of supporting the heavy field glasses. Below him, across the bay, the three Zeroes were lined up nose to tail. Japanese mechanics had been working on them for most of the afternoon. Jessop did not think that the aircraft would be taking off for Guadalcanal in the few remaining hours of daylight. Already the heat of the sun was diminishing. Soon canoes would be scudding out from the shelter of the island on fishing expeditions. Once he would have gone looking for bonito and kingfish with them, but that seemed a long time ago. Now things were different.

He heard footsteps crashing through the undergrowth and turned to see Sam Thomas lumbering up the hill through the trees. His enormous body, clad only in a lap-lap, was glistening with sweat.

1

Jessop watched him approach, idly wondering how much the giant weighed; it could hardly be less than sixteen stone.

'*Kai* time,' grunted Thomas as he drew near, jerking his head at the cluster of huts standing at the foot of the hill. 'Kumura and rice.'

Jessop frowned. For a moment he wondered whether to reprimand the half-caste, but finally decided against it. There was no point in antagonizing Thomas unless he had to. There might have to be confrontation one day, but the time was not yet ripe for it. Anyway he could not be sure that the man was being deliberately insubordinate. The rice would have been stolen from the Japanese. He had told Thomas before about the dangers of sending young men from the village across to the enemy lines on the mainland, but the big man always ignored the warnings. Bannion encouraged him, thought Jessop sourly, that was the trouble. Bannion encouraged him and Thomas believed that the sun shone out of the Australian.

'When are you going back to the camp?' he asked.

'Tonight,' answered Thomas, taking the field glasses and levelling them at the airstrip. 'Any messages?'

Jessop shook his head. As long as the batteries for his teleradio had been delivered there was nothing that Bannion could do for him. He glanced across the placid blue waters of the bay. Even without the aid of the field glasses he could still see the makeshift hangars and the patch of bare earth which served as a landing strip.

Over the last nine months, since the beginning of 1942, Jessop had watched the Japanese build and develop the small aerodrome on Renbanga. From his observation post on the tiny island less than a mile from the shore, he had noted the Japanese movements and passed them on to General Vandegrift and his Americans scrabbling desperately for a toehold on Guadalcanal.

Other coastwatchers in the Solomons, most of them pre-war planters and government officers, were similarly dotted about behind the Japanese lines, observing enemy shipping and aircraft movements and reporting them by radio: Kennedy on New Georgia, Clemens on Guadalcanal, Forster on Makira; Wilson, Bengough, Horton and a handful of others. Each man was alone, relying on Solomon Islanders to feed and shelter him.

'I won't be long,' said Jessop. He lingered, trying to think of something casual to say which would evoke a response from the other, but as usual nothing would come.

'No hurry,' said Thomas, not looking round.

Jessop nodded reluctantly and started down the slope, keeping to the remnants of the overgrown path between the trees, trying to avoid the creepers coiling treacherously underfoot. Although he was clad only in shorts and a shirt the perspiration coursed down his back. After four years in the Solomons he still had not grown accustomed to the heat and humidity.

Jessop's mind was not on his physical

discomfort. He was worrying about Thomas. Over the past few months there had been a perceptible change in the man's attitude. He still treated Jessop with the respect due a lieutenant from a sergeant in the Solomon Islands Defence Force, but Jessop was aware that such deference need mean nothing. Thomas spoke the language of his mother's people. On his visits to the island he could be expressing his contempt of the Englishman to the villagers. Perhaps Bannion had put him up to it; it was just the sort of thing he would do.

At the thought of the Australian Jessop experienced the familiar angry tightening in his stomach. Bloody man, he thought furiously. Bannion simply had no conception of duty, that was all there was to it. Only an Australian would flout his orders in such a fashion. His job, like Jessop's, was to keep an eye on the Japanese forces around Renbanga and the smaller islands in this part of the Protectorate, not to operate a personal task force. He should have been recalled in ignominy to Tulagi long ago. Instead, he was being treated by the authorities as if he was doing something wonderful. Just because that superannuated barge of his had blundered into an enemy torpedo boat in one of the inlets, and more by luck than judgement had managed to ram and sink it, Thomas, the bosun, had been awarded the Military Medal and Bannion given a free hand to prowl round the district. Meanwhile Jessop was stuck on this overgrown reef. It simply wasn't fair.

He realised that he was entering the village. Automatically his shoulders went back and his gait became more of a stride. The villagers sitting outside their thatched huts regarded him apathetically. Jessop did not speak to them. He had long ago resigned himself to the knowledge that he did not possess the gift of intimacy. Some district officers would have known exactly what to say without thinking. A sentence or two in language, or a brief joke, would have drawn instant laughter from the villagers. Jessop could not do this and the fact distressed him.

Apart from a few old crones minding the inevitable children there were few women to be seen. Most of them would be outside the village working in the gardens, tending the taro and kumura which made up the basic diet of these Melanesians. The men cleared the ground and planted the crops, then it was up to the women to cultivate the gardens and produce the food.

As he looked at the men sprawling in the shade of their huts Jessop strove to control his impatience. It was unfair to expect them to be energetic in this climate and with the high incidence of malaria. This little village nestling between the hill and the open sea differed only in detail from hundreds of others in the Solomons. As for the fact that the women did most of the work, well that was 'custom' and no European, whether he be government officer, missionary or trader, was going to change it.

Jessop turned sharply and walked between the huts, stepping over the babies playing on the ground among the scurrying chickens and yapping dogs. He stopped in front of a building of leaf and bamboo which was larger and more substantial than the others. Jessop stood gazing at it proprietorially. He did not allow himself to visit it more than once a day. This was his one success. If he had done nothing else during his nine months on the island he had argued and cajoled the villagers into building this. Now it was almost ready.

Abruptly Jessop walked back to the centre of the village, his face bearing no trace of the pleasure he felt. He looked past the group of huts to the sea. A hundred yards away the surf was breaking on the white sand of the beach. Canoes were drawn up on the beach, among them the one belonging to Thomas. Jessop searched among the idlers half-asleep in the sun until he saw the one he was looking for and then beckoned to him. A youth scrambled to his feet and ran towards the white man, grinning meaninglessly.

'Yes, master?' he asked eagerly.

'You come long Mr Sam long Kukala?' Jessop enquired.

'True now,' agreed the youth, nodding vigorously. He was about fourteen, tall

8

and lean. 'Mefella come allsame long Mr Sam.'

'You bring onefella Mary long youfella?' asked Jessop hopefully. 'Name bilong himi Miss Senda.'

'No, master,' declared the youth. 'No bringim onefella Mary.'

Jessop tried to hide his disappointment. He had been hoping that Senda would have come over from Kukala in the canoe with Thomas and Benny, the youth. He had sent for her as soon as he had heard that there was a mission-educated girl living on the mainland. That had been over a month ago. Even with the average Melanesian's lack of regard for time Senda should have been on her way by now. Something could have gone wrong. The uneasy smile on Benny's face urged him to go on probing.

'Whichway now?' asked Jessop. 'You gammon mefella? Me thinkim you catchim thisfella Mary some place.'

'Me no savvy,' said Benny wretchedly. He shuffled his feet and then burst out, 'Maybe me catchim thisfella Mary long Kukala.'

9

'At Kukala?' echoed Jessop, jolted out of his use of pidgin in his surprise. Kukala was Bannion's base, a small village on a natural anchorage farther down the coast of the main island of Renbanga. Senda had no business to be there.

'Him now,' acknowledged the boy. 'Himi stop long house bilong Master Bannion.'

Jessop stood quite still, masking his feelings. Bannion would never dare. He must have known that Senda was coming over to the island. He had no reason for delaying the girl. Or had he? Jessop realised that his hands were trembling. If this should prove another attempt on the Australian's part to make him look ridiculous he was not going to stand for it. This time the man had gone too far. Jessop glared at the now troubled Benny.

'You go quick time walkabout fetchim Mr Sam,' he ordered sharply.

Obediently the youth turned and started to scamper up the hill towards the oberservation-post, glad to get away. Slowly Jessop moved off in the direction of his hut. Although he was no longer hungry he would have to force himself to eat something.

★ ★ ★

It was pleasant in the shade of the palm tree, decided Thomas. He rested his massive shoulders against the trunk and stood lazily regarding the airstrip across the bay. Half a dozen Japanese mechanics were still crawling over the Zeroes, but the pilots were nowhere in sight and the general lack of urgency made it unlikely that the aircraft would fly today. There was seldom much activity in this part of the district, that was why Bannion left it alone. Occasionally a squadron of Mishtubi aircraft would land to refuel, while the three resident Zeroes flew now and again on scouting missions as far as Guadalcanal. For most of the time it was very quiet. Thomas wondered how Jessop stood the boredom and inactivity. No wonder the man was getting edgy; being stuck on this tiny rock was enough to drive a saint mad.

Unhurriedly the half-caste shifted his

position and rubbed his back reflectively against the tree. It was not easy for the Europeans who had volunteered to stay behind. Even Bannion was beginning to go through periods of brooding silence, in contrast to his normal cheerful manner. You could hardly blame them. Apart from a few sisters and priests Jessop and Bannion were the only whites in this part of the Solomons. They both knew that if the Japanese caught them they would be hanged as spies. It could hardly have a settling affect on their nerves.

Thomas yawned. He had no such worries. With his skin and features he could pass as a Melanesian any day, and his knowledge of the islands was sufficient to keep him out of the way of the Japanese should he and Bannion ever split up.

He had spent all his life among the islands, the son of a local girl and a footloose Welshman, one of the European misfits to be found in considerable numbers in the Pacific between the wars. Richard Thomas had been less avaricious than most, and after a series of unsuccessful careers as a gold-miner, trader and beach-comber had settled down contentedly enough to run a small plantation on land belonging to his wife's family.

Sam had been the eldest of six children and the only boy. He had inherited his mother's looks and pigmentation and his father's amiable disposition. As a half-breed he might have been treated with reserve or even outright antagonism were it not for the fact that while he was still in his teens Thomas, his slow-moving bulk belying his native shrewdness, loomed head and shoulders above the average Melanesian and could, if roused from his customary benevolent torpor, beat any two of them in a fight. Even the Tikopians, the toughest of all Solomon Islanders, treated Thomas with respect.

His position had been consolidated upon the death of his father. Richard Thomas fell from his canoe one night while on a solitary drunken fishing expedition and was drowned in Wanoni Bay. His son had inherited the plantation and thus as a landowner became a man of distinction in the eyes of the islanders.

After this the half-caste scarcely needed the added security brought about by his marriage into the most powerful family in the district, for which privilege he paid the almost unprecedented bride-price of ten pigs, twenty pounds in cash, a case of whisky and a fathom of Santa Cruz red feather money. However, Thomas was basically a cautious man and regarded the extra insurance as well worth the price he had paid for it.

By the time of the Japanese invasion Thomas, who was twenty-eight, was the undisputed leading man around Renbanga and had been heard of as far away as Vanikoro in the east and Ontong Java in the north. His plantation was one of the few to show a profit during the era of the slump in world copra prices, and a string of village trading stores did a flourishing business, even allowing for the rake-off deducted at source by those relatives who insisted on being put in charge.

Upon the outbreak of war Thomas had thrown in his lot with the British administration, reasoning that despite the reverses being suffered in the Pacific by the white men, they must in the long run prove too strong for the Japanese.

But over the last few months the situation had changed. The white man was no longer all-powerful. The myth of his supremacy had been shattered in the eyes of the islanders. They had seen the British and Australians fleeing in confusion from the Japanese, giving up with hardly a struggle an empire which had been theirs for forty years. The Americans recently arrived on Guadalcanal were having to fight and die for every yard of ground they gained, while only a month ago the cruisers *Astoria*, *Vincennes* and *Quincy* had been sunk in Solomons waters by Japanese surface vessels. Things were not good, thought Thomas.

For some moments he had been conscious of someone running up the hill behind him. Judging by the speed and lightness of the footsteps it would be Benny. The boy seldom left Thomas alone for more than a few hours. To all intents and purposes the boy had adopted the half-caste, following him wherever he went. At first Thomas had tried to drive the youth away. The latter came from a village on the far side of Renbanga and was not even a one-talk of the big man so had no claim on him. But Benny had persisted in making himself so useful that eventually Thomas had given way. Now, although he would not admit it, he would miss having the boy paddling his canoe and preparing their food.

'D.O. want for speakim long you,' panted the boy as he approached. 'Himi say go-go quick time now.'

Thomas levered himself away from the tree. Now what was the matter, he wondered resignedly. It was becoming more trouble than it was worth bringing Jessop his radio batteries and other occasional supplies. Without a word he handed the field glasses to Benny, gesturing at the Zeroes on the airstrip. Eagerly the boy seized the glasses and raised them to his eyes, directing his gaze at the airfield, his whole body rigid with pride and concentration. Thomas left him scrutinising the airstrip as if his life depended on it.

By the time Thomas reached the village again the women were coming in from the gardens and were carrying jugs and buckets to the stream to draw water for the evening meal. Some of them carried containers of hollowed-out bamboo. The women were bare-breasted, clad in tattered skirts faded from many washings. Thomas was careful not to look too closely at the younger ones as he passed them. With the solitary exception of land disputes there was nothing more likely to cause a lasting blood-feud than a suspicion that an outsider had paid more than cursory attention to a wife or daughter. Thomas always respected the customs and tabus of a village; it was one of the reasons for his success. Each area had its own superstitions and beliefs and these changed every few miles. Although there were less than a hundred and fifty thousand people in the Solomons, over sixty different languages were spoken; often the people of neighbouring villages were unable to understand each other.

Thomas walked to the hut occupied by

Jessop. The Japanese seldom visited the unimportant island. When they did the district officer always received enough warning to take to the bush until the patrol had left. Thomas ducked his head and entered the main room of the hut. There were few furnishings, merely a camp-bed and a makeshift table. An oil lamp was suspended from the rafters. Jessop was squatting on the beaten earth floor, spooning kumura and rice from a battered mess-tin. When he saw Thomas he nodded and pointed to the ground before him.

'Sit down, sergeant,' he invited pleasantly. 'I'll be with you as soon as I've finished my dinner.'

Impassively Thomas lowered himself to the floor and watched as Jessop ran his spoon round the inside of the tin. Although it had been the greater part of a year since the Englishman had been landed on the island at night, Jessop still managed to look trim. His khaki shorts and shirt, although wrinkled and sweat-stained, hung neatly on his lean form. He had retained his long regulation socks and service boots in defiance of the climate. With his pink and white complexion which refused to tan, and his clear blue eyes, Jessop looked oddly vulnerable and innocent, younger even than his twenty-six years. Only the slight intermittent twitching of one eye betrayed the tension and strain he was under.

'Well now,' declared the district officer. He put his mess-tin down carefully and licked his spoon clean before replacing it in the tin. 'Well now,' he repeated.

Thomas waited patiently. The other man would get to the point sooner or later. The Englishman smiled, a mere contortion of his lips to reveal teeth that were large and white. There was no mirth in his eyes.

'I'm not very happy,' he said in a plaintive tone.

Thomas nodded encouragingly. He had long ago learned never to pay any attention to the words used by a white man but to search for the sense behind them, like a man diving for shells off an unknown reef. The half-caste could tell that Jessop was not angry with him.

Instead there was a stiffness in his voice, a mixture of embarrassment and wounded pride which indicated that a third party was going to be discussed, much against Jessop's will. Bannion, decided the big man; it had to be Bannion. Jessop had never criticised the Australian aloud before, but everyone knew that they detested each other. Thomas tried to compose his features into an expression of judicious sympathy as he waited for his superior officer to go on.

Jessop coughed. 'As you know, Sergeant Thomas, we have recently built a village school and arranged for a girl from Renbanga to come and teach in it.'

'Yes, sir.'

'I understand that Miss Senda, our new school-mistress, has been seen at Kukala,' he said carefully.

Benny had been talking, thought Thomas. Inwardly he cursed the youth's loose tongue. He could sense trouble, and no native with any sense got involved in a white man's quarrel.

'I think so, sir,' he answered. 'Major Bannion asked her to stay behind.'

'Indeed?' asked Jessop coolly. 'Did he give any reason for this rather unusual request?'

'No, sir.'

'You can throw no light on the matter?'

'No, sir.'

'I see. Thank you, sergeant. That's all.'

'Yes, sir,' said Thomas with alacrity, grateful that the interview was over. He stood up. 'I'll see you again when I come over with the battries and supplies next month.'

'You'll see me before that, Sergeant Thomas,' said Jessop grimly. 'I'm coming to Kukala with you tonight.'

2

Clouds swirled madly across the night sky. Sometimes they obscured the moon and then the sea became black and bottomless. Thomas and Benny paddled economically but with deceptive power, guiding the canoe past the dark outline of the coast of Renbanga. Although they had been travelling for the last three hours they were showing no signs of strain. From his position in the prow of the craft Jessop gave occasional token assistance, but his awkward efforts were scarcely needed.

They had left the airstrip and its detachment of support troops behind them. There were other Japanese garrisons stationed along the shore but these were small and not very efficiently manned. The fighting on Guadalcanal was more than a hundred miles away; the troops on Renbanga had no reason to be particularly alert. The main danger tonight would come from any enemy patrol vessels cruising in the area, but these would not usually bother with a solitary nocturnal canoe.

Jessop twisted in his seat to get a better view of the wooded slopes sprawling down to the beach. From these inlets in the old days the Renbanga warriors had set off in their long decorated war canoes, hunting for slaves and trophies as far as Choiseul in one direction and Malaita in the other. Later the descendants of these same warriors had become the pursued, fleeing inland from the notorious black-birders, Australian schooners kidnapping native labour for the sugar plantations of Queensland and Fiji.

Even then the men had shown their innate fighting ability. The first labour recruiting vessels had things much their own way, but by the time later ships appeared the Melanesians knew what to expect and were prepared. More than one Australian landing-party had been massacred on the beach and the islands had received the sobriquet of the savage Solomons.

The islanders were still warriors, thought Jessop. Just because they had taken little part in the present conflict the Americans were writing them off as timid bushmen. This was far from being the case. The Melanesians were bewildered by the war and unable to understand what it was all about. The majority had had little or no contact with the pre-war British administration and had never heard of America or Japan. The fighting on Guadalcanal mystified them.

Jessop was roused from his reverie by a change in the direction of the canoe. Glancing over his shoulder he saw that Thomas was digging his paddle repeatedly into the water on the port side, swinging the craft towards the shore. To a casual onlooker the approaching beach differed little from the coast they had been passing for the past few hours. As they drew closer, however, a fissure appeared in what had apparently been a sheer rock face. The opening was almost entirely obscured by overhanging trees and mangrove creepers. Gently the canoe nosed its way into the opening, both

Thomas and Benny raising their paddles.

Jessop leaned forward to avoid the thickly trailing branches and creepers. It was very quiet in the tunnel formed by the foliage dipping and swooping above the placid water like the wings of a dark and monstrous bird. Now that they were inside the entrance the full size of the creek became apparent. It was thirty feet from bank to bank and Jessop knew that the depth of the water was sufficient to float any of the vessels in Bannion's makeshift fleet.

As if at a signal Thomas and Benny began paddling in unison, urging the canoe round a bend. There the inlet widened into a natural harbour completely hidden from the sea. The dense undergrowth on three sides added to the sense of desolation.

The Englishman strained his eyes to peer through the gloom. Somewhere ahead of them would be the wooden wharf constructed by Bannion and his native labourers. He could just make out the dim shape of Bannion's almost derelict trading vessel, the *Nancy*, shifting complainingly at anchor, while several barges rescued from an abandoned plantation crouched in a squat and ungainly fashion like frogs just above the water line.

On the shore, beyond the wharf which could now be distinguished, were a few native huts. Thomas steered the canoe while Benny jumped ashore and held the canoe steady for Jessop to step on to the wooden structure of the wharf. As he did so a figure clad only in a pair of ragged trousers rolled up to his calves moved forward carrying a lantern.

'Stone me if the bloody mountain hasn't come to Mahomet,' said the figure sardonically.

Jessop nodded stiffly. 'Hullo, Bannion,' he said.

The Australian looked over Jessop's shoulder at Thomas who was methodically securing the canoe to the wharf. 'Everything all right, Tommo?' he asked. 'You haven't flogged your medal to the Japs yet?'

'Not yet, boss,' replied the half-caste equably.

'You better hadn't,' grunted Bannion. 'You want to hang on to it, mate. You may need it to drape over your whatsits when your shorts fall to pieces.' He swung round on Jessop. 'I can't get over this,' he marvelled. 'Social calls yet. Come on up to the house.'

Jessop followed the other man along the jetty. The cool night air struck against his face. Various islanders who had appeared melted back into the darkness, their curiosity assuaged. Bannion moved busily ahead, a short, broad-shouldered man inclined to plumpness. He moved jerkily as if controlling his natural energy with a considerable effort. Leaving the jetty he led Jessop to a hut standing a little to one side of the others in a clearing hacked out of the bush.

'Come on in,' he invited, ducking his head in order to get through the door. 'It ain't much, but it's home.'

The solitary room inside the hut was large and sparsely furnished. Most of the space was taken up by a ramshackle table. An oil-lamp hanging from a wall illuminated a scale map of Renbanga spread out on the table. Bannion rolled up the map and threw it into a corner. Then he stooped and produced a bottle of whisky from a box underneath his chair.

'This is quite an occasion,' he remarked drily. 'I reckon we can drink to it.' He peered at Jessop. 'Unless, that is, you've come to serve another bloody summons on me.'

Jessop flushed. On several occasions before the war during his first tour of duty in the Solomons he had fined the Australian for breaches of the regulations. Bannion had been an itinerant trader, running his dilapidated schooner from harbour to harbour, picking up occasional cargoes of copra in exchange for tinned foods, tobacco and, it was suspected, illicit alcohol. Bannion had been a nuisance, one of those wandering, irresponsible colonials sent, it sometimes seemed, specially to plague British administrators. Now the man was a hero. For someone of Jessop's tidy turn of mind it was both annoying and confusing.

'This is an official call,' he said quickly. One had to get things straight with

28

Bannion from the outset, otherwise the man dodged about all over the place with that misplaced sense of humour of his.

The Australian paused in the act of adding water from a bottle to the two glasses of whisky before him. 'I thought it might be,' he observed drily after a pause, and went on pouring the water, his mobile, comedian's features blank.

Jessop nodded, satisfied that he had made his point. He waited in silence until one of the glasses had been thrust across the table at him. Then he raised his glass almost primly to his lips. 'Cheers,' he said self-consciously.

'Bottoms up,' acknowledged Bannion briefly.

Jessop replaced the glass on the table after a token sip. He did not like the taste of alcohol and normally did not touch it. To have refused on this occasion, however, would probably have sparked off one of Bannion's caustic remarks and almost inevitably feeling would have entered the discussion. Jessop did not care for scenes; he did not flinch from their emotional content but deplored them for the inefficiency they engendered.

'Another?' asked Bannion, draining his glass and refilling it. He looked at the level in the district officer's glass. 'What's the matter?' he asked caustically. 'Training for a return match with Cambridge?'

For the hundredth time Jessop wished that the High Commissioner had never revealed that his latest junior recruit had been an Oxford athletics blue. Over the last four years it had provided too much ammunition for people like Bannion. Cautiously he cast about in his mind for a way of broaching the matter which had brought him to Kukala. Before he could speak the Australian forestalled him.

'Anyway, I'm glad you're here. I've got a proposition to put to you,' he said roughly.

'Indeed?'

'That's right.' Bannion's eyes were fixed on Jessop now, light-blue and unblinking. Jessop shifted uneasily. What crack-brained project was about to be proposed? Really, these people were the end. He had seen so many of them as a cadet-officer before the war. They drifted from island to island with no thought for the future; drinking, wenching and brawling as the fancy took them. There had been that Irishman up in New Guinea a few years ago that they all talked about, the one who was acting in Hollywood films now; what was his name — Errol Flynn. He had only been one of a hundred hell-raisers like Bannion.

With a start of annoyance Jessop realised that his attention had been wandering. That was one of the draw-backs to being on his own so much. His mind went off at tangents with the ease of a compulsive talker embracing a fresh subject. He glanced apologetically at Bannion.

'I'm sorry,' he said. 'I didn't quite . . . '

With an obvious effort Bannion con-trolled his impatience. 'I said that it's time we got off our backsides and did something constructive,' he repeated harshly.

'Our orders are to keep out of the way

and observe,' Jessop pointed out automatically. 'They're quite definite on that score — .'

'Orders!' Bannion's voice was abrasive. 'A bloody lot of use orders are to us down here. Hell's bells, man, we're on our own. Nobody can tell us what to do.'

'I disagree. We were sent to Renbanga for a purpose. If there was any change in plans we'd be told.'

Bannion's contemptuous glare was malevolent in its intensity. 'They've really got you trained to jump through hoops, haven't they?' he asked softly. 'Yes sir, no sir, three bags full sir. You keep this up and you'll get your flaming knighthood, my oath you will.'

Jessop allowed himself a cool smile. Such an outburst was only to be expected from the volatile Australian. Calmly he looked round the room. The swinging oil-lamp barely illuminated the centre of the hut and abandoned the rest to darkness, an area of deep and shifting shadows. Small winged insects hovered avariciously about the shining glass while other creatures could be heard scampering round the bamboo walls. Motionless above the table the faces of both men seemed yellow and blotchy.

'At least listen to me,' pleaded Bannion, exasperation tinting his voice. Jessop shrugged unwillingly and the Australian took a deep breath. 'I reckon we ought to go for something big,' he declared vehemently in a rush of words. 'That airstrip you're watching — why don't we put it out of action?'

'The airstrip?' Jessop controlled himself and gave Bannion a faintly pitying smile. 'You're joking.'

'Sure, I'm wearing a funny hat as well,' retorted Bannion bitterly. He leant across the table until his face was close to Jessop's. The latter could see small globules of spittle forming on the Australian's lips. 'If we play our cards right we could move in, wreck that airstrip and the Zeroes, and be away before they knew what had hit 'em.'

'It's out of the question,' declared Jessop unhesitatingly. 'You must be mad.

We mustn't commit ourselves. We've got a watching brief here. If we start making raids we'll lose all our effectiveness.'

'Oh for God's sake!' expostulated Bannion angrily.

'I see no point in continuing this discussion,' snapped Jessop. 'I intend carrying out my instructions and they don't include making ridiculous punitive expeditions.'

'What do you want to do?' demanded Bannion. 'Spend the rest of the war sitting on that rock of yours? Is that what you want?'

'I'll do it if I have to.'

'Look,' said Bannion. 'Look, I know we don't get on but we're the only two white men for hundreds of miles. I need you for this expedition.'

'Then you're not getting me. The whole point of our being here is that the Japanese don't know where we are. If we start making ourselves too trouble-some they're going to come looking for us. That means we won't be able to relay any information back to Guadalcanal.'

'You mean you haven't got the guts,' said Bannion.

The two men stared in silence at each other. 'I came here for something else,' said Jessop eventually. 'I understand that you have a Miss Senda Tozaka staying in the village.'

'Who?' After a moment Bannion's puzzled expression cleared. 'Oh, you mean the mission girl. Yes, she's here somewhere. What about it?'

'She has no business being here,' said Jessop. 'We're waiting for her at the village school.'

'You've come all this way just to tell me that? In the middle of a bloody war?'

'War or no war I've a duty to the people of my district. We've built the school and now we're waiting for Senda to come and teach there.'

'You know what you are, don't you?' asked Bannion furiously. 'You're too bloody good to live.'

Jessop did not answer. He stood a little to one side of the table, as politely bored and detached as a waiter. Bannion glowered up at him.

'You've got a nerve,' he went on. 'You Poms are all the same; no good to man or beast.'

'Just because I want a teacher for my school?'

'Suppose I won't let her go?' demanded Bannion roughly.

'You don't understand,' said Jessop patiently. 'I've come to fetch her. I've no intention of leaving without that girl.'

Bannion was suddenly still, his putty-like face blank and dangerous. In spite of his resolution Jessop experienced a moment of cold apprehension. He wondered if he had driven the Australian too far. Bannion was all-powerful here in Kukala; no man told him what to do. That was half the trouble, thought Jessop with a spurt of anger, the local people had treated Bannion for too long as a little tin god. It was time somebody stood up to him.

'Well?' he asked curtly. 'Are you going to send for the girl, or aren't you?'

'You're pushing it, mate,' Bannion declared flatly. 'It wouldn't take much to make me hang one on you.'

'I'm not interested,' Jessop told him. 'You're hanging on to this girl just to annoy me. I'm taking her back with me tonight.'

'I'm what?' asked Bannion incredulously. 'Listen, sport, if I wanted to annoy you I could think of a lot of better ways of doing it, believe you me.'

'Then why — ' began Jessop, only to stop when he realised what the other man meant.

'Why don't you grow up?' asked Bannion. 'Why else do you think I'd keep her?'

'I see,' said Jessop stiffly. 'Well, I hope you're proud of yourself.'

'It doesn't matter all that much to me,' said Bannion wearily. 'I don't reckon on being made captain of the school anyway. Look, son, she's just another abo, that's all. A bit prettier and cleaner than some, maybe, but no different.'

Jessop tried to conceal his chagrin. So that was why Bannion was delaying the girl at Kukala; he had installed her in the harem he was reputed to maintain. Jessop felt humiliated at his own lack of perception. He should have known better than to let Senda make her journey via Kukala in the first place.

'I'm sorry to break up the happy home,' he said curtly. 'We need her at the school.'

'God save the king,' sighed Bannion. 'The Japs are practically pissing in your ear and all you can think about is a sodding school.'

'It happens to be part of my job. This was my district before the war.'

'Your district,' said Bannion scathingly. 'Don't come it with me, son. You were just a big white cowboy poncing about on a big white horse. You were here about five minutes and thought you knew it all.'

'At least I didn't sell the natives alcohol and interfere with their women,' retorted Jessop. He raised his voice to drown Bannion's reply. 'We're getting away from the point. I'm waiting for that girl.'

'Don't put down roots,' snarled the Australian.

'I'm perfectly prepared to submit an official complaint,' said Jessop.

'You would, too,' agreed Bannion,

staring hard at the district officer. 'At a time like this you'd stir it for me if you felt like it.'

'That's right.'

Bannion's shoulders slumped. 'Oh, dry your eyes,' he said irritably. 'You can have the bloody woman. There's plenty more where she came from. These blacks like getting poked by a white man.'

'People like you ought to be run out of the Protectorate,' said Jessop furiously, before he could restrain himself.

Bannion crashed his glass down on the table and strode round the table until he was standing in front of the district officer, quivering like a pointer. 'I've told you before,' he said tensely. 'Watch that mouth of yours, Jessop. It's going to get you into trouble one day.'

'I'll have to risk that, won't I?'

Without a word Bannion turned and hurried out of the hut. When he had gone Jessop sat down gratefully. His legs were shaking slightly. He had outfaced the Australian on this occasion but he was not anxious to repeat the experience. A sudden wave of impatience washed over the district officer. It was all the girl's fault! If she had come straight to the island none of this would have happened. Instead she had stayed to sniff around Bannion like a bitch on heat. The sooner she was taken out to the school and put to work the better it would be for everyone.

Jessop wondered what the girl would be like. All that he knew about her was what he had heard from Thomas and one or two village headmen. She was supposed to be eighteen, unmarried and had been educated at a Methodist mission near Munda. After that she had stayed on as an assistant teacher. The European missionaries had been flown out at the time of the Japanese invasion and the mission station abandoned. The girl was probably spoiled, thought Jessop; he knew the sort, a bright Melanesian child petted and made much of by the missionaries until she grew up and became insufferable, too good for her own race and feebly aping the ways of the white people who had deprived her of her culture.

Jessop looked at his watch. It was ten

o'clock. It would take at least four hours to get back to the island so it was time he left. He stood up and moved outside the hut. Automatically he brushed off the mosquitoes and stood looking about him in the moonlight. The clearing extended on all three sides of the head of the inlet. Groups of huts were scattered about. One or two dark forms were moving about quietly. For all the air of desolation Jessop knew that the area was well guarded. Bannion had spent a great deal of time looking for a suitable base and now that he had found one he was going to look after it. Not only was the anchorage hidden from the sea, the inlet was big enough to allow an American flying-boat to land.

'Jessop!' Bannion's voice crackled derisively through the night. 'Your woman's here.'

The district officer looked in the direction of the voice. Bannion was standing outside one of the huts, a girl at his side. She was tall for a Melanesian and held herself with dignity. As she drew closer the plain cotton dress could not disguise her firm breasts and shapely figure. Her features, which were fine and regular, were set in an expression of watchful repose. Bannion had been right, thought Jessop reluctantly, by any standards this girl was beautiful. He dismissed the thought and nodded aloofly.

'Good-evening. Name bilong me Mister Jessop. Mebbe you savvy — '

'I have heard of you, Mr Jessop,' said the girl in a voice which was low and cool.

And you're too grand to use pidgin, registered Jessop. All right, my lady, if that's the way you want it. Aloud he said.

'I want to get back to my island tonight. Are you ready to travel now?'

'I'm ready.' Jessop noticed that the girl was carrying a sleeping-mat and a small woven bag which presumably contained her possessions.

'I'm letting you have Benny,' interrupted Bannion, his voice harsh and indifferent. 'He'll help row you back. Senda can take an oar as well.'

The three of them walked down to the

jetty. Benny was waiting by a canoe, his teeth gleaming in a delighed smile. Senda did not look at Bannion as she climbed into the canoe and took her place in the middle. Jessop stopped and faced the Australian.

'About your project,' he said awkwardly. 'I'm sorry I couldn't — '

'Don't give it another thought,' said Bannion heavily. 'You've got much more important things to think about, *Mr* Jessop.'

Jessop shrugged and scrambled down into the prow of the canoe. Benny jumped off the wharf into the waist-deep water and pushed the canoe away from the jetty before jumping back in and taking up his paddle. Bannion stood and watched the canoe until it had turned the bend of the creek. Then he turned and walked back towards his hut.

3

Senda made her attempt to escape an hour after they had left Kukala. They had been paddling silently through the choppy seas a mile off the coast of Renbanga when the girl suddenly jack-knifed over the side of the canoe. Jessop heard the splash as she hit the water, followed by Benny's gasp of astonishment. Then Senda's dark head was bobbing above the waves ten yards away.

Jessop cursed and scooped his oar vigorously into the water, swinging the canoe precariously towards the shore. Recovering from his surprise Benny joined his efforts to those of the district officer. The canoe lurched over the jostling waves as its occupants paddled frantically.

Under normal circumstances the canoe would never have caught up with the swimming girl, but tonight there was a strong off-shore current beating out from the island. The swell began to catch Senda and hurl her back. Benny could handle a canoe skilfully and over a short distance Jessop was wiry enough to keep pace with him. The canoe, buffeted from side to side and shipping water, gained on Senda. Once she turned and trod water painfully, shaking her head spaniel-like and panting for breath as she squinted without hope at her pursuers. When she twisted round on to her stomach again her strokes were slower and less assured.

Jessop shouted to Benny to increase speed. The canoe drew level with Senda. She tried to change direction but most of her strength had gone. Jessop reached over the side and grabbed her by the hair. Desperately Benny shifted his paddle from side to side in an effort to keep the craft upright. The girl screamed as Jessop dragged her out of the water. Jessop moved his grip to her shoulders and then secured her by the waist, heaving her into the bottom of the canoe where she writhed feebly like a landed fish.

'Sit up,' snarled Jessop, his lips tight with anger. 'Come on, sit up.'

For a moment he thought that the girl was going to ignore him but slowly she hauled herself into a sitting position. She was still sobbing for breath and even though Jessop could not see her face he could sense Senda's terror.

'Pick up that oar and row,' he commanded tersely. 'We'll sort this out later. Benny, spose thisfella Senda go-go, you killem long paddle, savvy?'

'Yes, master,' said Benny, his voice without expression in the gloom.

Jessop stood glowering at the girl until, her body racked with choking sobs, she picked up her paddle and began dipping it in the water. Then he took his place in the prow of the canoe with his back to the other two. Under Benny's guidance the craft with his back to the other two. Under Benny's guidance the craft veered round until once again it was parallel with the coast. As Jessop crouched in the bows he controlled his fury. He would discover the reason for Senda's behaviour later. At the moment he was concerned only with getting away from the area before any onlooker on the shore should become interested in the erratic manoeuvrings of the craft.

It was not until they had been paddling for another quarter of an hour that they heard the engines. Benny's sharp ears caught the sound first and his low whistle alerted Jessop. The district officer had to wait another thirty seconds before he could hear the ominous stutter, faint at first but drawing closer.

'An aeroplane?' he hazarded.

'No more. Twofella boat,' corrected Benny authoritatively. 'Bilong Japani. Himi come quick time.'

Jessop shipped his oar and tried to think. He was perplexed. To have two Japanese patrol boats scouring the area at this time of night was unusual.

'Which way?' he asked.

Benny's finger pointed unerringly to the east. Jessop strained his eyes. In the distance he could just make out two faint semi-circles of light, little bigger than pin-pricks.

'Searchlights,' he said. 'They're looking for something.' He came to a decision and indicated the small bay they were

47

passing. 'You catchem Japani this place?' he asked the youth.

'No, master. No catchem Japani.'

Jessop nodded. It was too dangerous to stay out at sea if the Japanese were launching a search. It would be safer to put in to the shore and shelter among the undergrowth until the patrol boats had passed.

'That way,' he ordered, indicating the bay. 'Waitem short time.'

Benny murmured assent and edged the canoe in the direction of the bay. They paddled cautiously, negotiating a sand-bank across the mouth of the inlet. When they were thirty yards from the beach Benny leapt out up to his chest in the water and began pushing the canoe. When the water was at waist level Jessop and Senda scrambled out of the dug-out and helped the youth drag it up the shelving crescent of the beach flanked by the inevitable lowering jungle of trees and undergrowth. They reached the edge of the clearing and at a word from Jessop busied themselves in covering the canoe with branches and palm fronds. When this had been accomplished the three of them stood in the shelter of the trees, staring out to sea.

'Close up now,' said Benny.

Jessop did not bother to reply. The patrol boats were almost immediately off the coast. It was obvious that they were quartering the area methodically, sweeping round in intersecting arcs. The sandbank prevented them from entering the bay but on several occasions the searchlights raked the beach severely. The vessels seemed to remain in the area for an interminable time but when they had finally passed on down the coast Jessop turned to Benny.

'You savvy this place ia, Benny?' he asked.

Benny nodded eagerly. 'True now,' he affirmed. 'Line bilong me catchem house close up this place.'

Jessop was relieved. If Benny had relatives in the vicinity it simplified things. They did not dare put out to sea again with the Japanese boats prowling around, so he might as well find out what the panic was about.

'You go-go quick time now findem whichway Japani lookim,' he instructed. 'Me waitem long you.'

Needing no second bidding Benny hurried away into the undergrowth. Reluctantly Jessop faced Senda. He had enough on his mind without her but he had to find out the reason for her flight from the canoe. He was about to question her when he noticed that the girl was shivering through her sodden dress.

'You'd better get your clothes off before you catch pneumonia,' Jessop told her roughly.

The girl stared sullenly at him. Her eyes were momentarily vulnerable and then hardened like steel being forged under fire. Slowly she drew up her dress, sleeking it over her head and dropping it to the sand. She was wearing nothing else. She stood naked before Jessop, the full brown plenitude of her body revealed.

'Which way now, master?' she asked bitterly, using the pidgin like an edged weapon. 'You wanem black girl lie down for you? Mebbe you wanem — '

'For God's sake!' burst out Jessop. 'What the hell are you playing at?' He goggled at the dark-tipped breasts and the shadows playing on the polished skin, and even in his confusion he thought that he had never seen anything so beautiful. 'Put your clothes on,' he instructed harshly, hurriedly averting his gaze.

'You don't want me?' he heard the girl ask incredulously.

'Of course not. Put your dress on.'

He waited until Senda had had time to pull the dress back over her head and then swung round. The girl was looking disturbed and unsure of herself.

'What's this all about?' he demanded. 'What made you jump overboard?'

'I thought you would be like the other one,' said Senda hesitantly.

'The other — ? You mean Bannion?'

'That's right. The other white master.' The words were so biting that Jessop almost flinched at their impact.

'Did he — ?'

'He pleasured me; I think that is the phrase.'

'I'm sorry,' said Jessop after a pause.

'Do you want to bring a charge of rape against him?'

'What would be the point? Don't you know, Mr Jessop? You can't rape a nig-nog. They all enjoy it. Especially from a white man.'

'We aren't all like Bannion.'

'No.' For a moment the girl's tone softened. 'The missionaries were good to me.' The iron entered her tone again. 'You could almost make a score out of it, like a football match. One goal to the mission people, one to Bannion.'

'You speak English very well,' was all Jessop could think of to say.

'I was a good student. The missionaries were going to send me to a college in Fiji, but the war stopped that. Now I'm a bush girl again.' The note of bitterness came back. 'Onefella jig-jig Mary bilong white man.'

'I'll see that Bannion faces a charge,' promised Jessop hotly. 'It may have to wait until the war's over — '

'No more,' interrupted Senda impatiently. She hesitated, searching for words, and then went on, 'It's white man's custom to take local girls. Planters and traders have always done it.'

Jessop felt lost and inadequate. There was a great deal of truth in Senda's statement. Before the war British jurisdiction in the districts had been in the hands of a few scattered district officers, each responsible for hundreds of square miles of territory. Some expatriates had taken advantage of this lack of supervision and had regarded themselves as beyond the law.

'What you say is true,' he admitted, choosing his words carefully. 'But things will be different one day. Solomon islanders will look after themselves and make their own laws. But they will have to be educated first. People like you will have to teach them. You can do that now. Come and teach at my school. Nobody will interfere with you, I can promise that.'

The girl's eyes searched his face. Then she nodded as if satisfied with what she saw. 'I'll teach at your school, Mr Jessop.' For the first time she smiled. 'Anyway, I don't have much choice. I come from

Vella Lavella. Now that the missionaries have gone I'm a stranger here.'

'You won't be a stranger on the island,' Jessop assured her. 'You'll be more than welcome.' He glanced at his watch, relieved that one problem had been solved. 'Now all we've got to do is wait for Benny.'

It was another thirty minutes before the youth returned. Jessop and Senda sat on a fallen tree trunk. They did not speak. Unbidden a picture of the girl's naked body came into the district officer's mind and he struggled to dismiss it. A wind shuffled through the palm trees overhead. Waves washed languidly along the beach. It was hard to remember that a hundred miles away on Guadalcanal Americans and Japanese alike were being slaughtered on similar beaches.

When Benny came back he slipped through the trees so silently that even though Jessop had been straining to hear him, the first he knew of the boy's approach was when he actually materialised out of the shadows. Benny was looking excited.

'Did you find somebody?' asked Jessop quickly.

'Yes, master,' nodded the youth. 'Me talk-talk long man bilong village. Himi say one fella bird, him gottim onefella engine, go-go fallim long sky.'

'An aeroplane crashed near here? Bilong Japani?'

'No, master. Allsame bilong 'Merican. Onefella man bilong bird, himi fall down.'

Jessop listened intently with growing excitement as the boy rattled on. Slowly the district officer pieced Benny's disjointed tale together. An American single-seater aircraft, probably a Seagull, had made a crash landing somewhere along the coast that afternoon. The pilot had been rescued by some villagers and spirited away into the bush. Now the Japanese, who must have heard the crash, were searching for the aeroplane and its pilot. When Benny had finished and was looking expectantly at the district officer Jessop stood thinking.

'Thisfella 'Merican — himi close up?'

'No, master. Himi mebbe three hours,

mebbe five hours away. Plenty safe long bush.'

That made sense. The Japanese would be searching the villages. It would go hard on any Melanesians found harbouring an American pilot. It had been a good idea to take the pilot up into the bush.

'You savvy this place good?'

'Yes, master. Me savvy plenty good.'

Jessop blessed the fact that Bannion had given him a local boy as a guide. His duty was plain. He would have to find the American and arrange for him to be returned to Guadalcanal. That meant that he had to get to the pilot's lair before the Japanese search-parties.

'We go quick time,' he assured Benny. He turned to Senda. 'I must go and find this pilot. He's some way off. Do you want to wait here while Benny and I go and look for him?'

'No,' said Senda emphatically. 'I'll come with you.' She noticed the district officer's doubtful expression. 'Don't worry, Mr Jessop,' she said mockingly. 'I'll keep up with you.'

* * *

The overgrown trail sloped sharply upwards as Benny led the way towards the centre of Renbanga. Jessop leaned forward, pumping for breath and struggling up the incline. In accordance with Melanesian tradition the girl followed some distance behind. She moved easily and without apparent strain. They had been walking, with several short breaks, for over four hours.

The trees blotted out the moon but in the darkness Benny's judgement was unerring. He struck a way for them through the waist-high matted undergrowth with a bush knife he had borrowed from a village at the beginning of the track.

Jessop tried to forget his aching legs and searing lungs by concentrating his thoughts on other things. There had been other walks, ones that now seemed part of a different world. He remembered the strolls along the gull-swooping cliffs of the Isle of Wight where he had grown up, the solitary, introspective son of a local minister. These had been followed by several walking tours on the continent in the university vacations. Germany he had particularly liked, and he had witnessed and been saddened by the blatant stirrings of Nazi militarism.

Jessop had made few friends at Oxford but his pleasant and unassuming manner had secured him tolerance, and it was with some surprise that his acquaintances had witnessed his sudden translation to a minor glory as the second-string miler for the university.

His decision to enter the Colonial Service and to opt for a posting to the Solomon Islands had not been a sudden whim. Jessop had made up his mind some time before he had taken his Third in History. The idea of a life in the South Pacific had appealed to him. Grimble's books about the Gilbert and Ellice Islands had been a part of his adolescence and he had gone on to read everything he could about that part of the world.

The Solomons had always had a great attraction for him ever since he had Amherst's translation of the accounts of

Mendana's expedition to the unknown islands in 1568. The account of the landing on Santa Isabel, written down by an unknown sailor, had lodged in Jessop's memory.

⋆　⋆　⋆

And the sailor reported land, and presently it was visible to us. And we hoisted a flag and everybody received the news with great joy and gratitude for the grace that God had vouchsafed to us through the intercession of the Virgin of Good Fortune, the Glorious Mother of God, whom we all worshipped, to whom we all prayed, singing the Te Deum Laudamus.

⋆　⋆　⋆

The Spaniards had almost been wrecked on a reef as they approached Santa Isabel, and the sailor had gone on to say.

⋆　⋆　⋆

We had recourse to prayers and petitions according to the custom of navigators when they are in danger as we were at that moment. Then the wind shifted and although it was ten o'clock in the morning a star appeared over the tree tops and guided us to safety.

* * *

The star had probably been the planet Venus which sometimes appears in the day in Pacific latitudes, but the Spaniards were convinced that they had been saved by a miracle. To Mendana's sailors the Solomons must have seemed a haven after their hazardous voyage across the Pacific. In succeeding centuries the islands had proved a similar refuge for many other white men; seamen, traders, beachcombers, missionaries and then Government officers had all made homes there. When Jessop had arrived as a cadet in 1938 he had found the place and the people to be as attractive as he had hoped.

Although the islands could hardly be

called attractive now, he thought grimly as he trudged after Benny. The Japanese occupied the western and central districts, including Guadalcanal, while their ships, after the American defeat at Ironbottom Sound, controlled the waters off all the islands. Most Europeans had fled at the first approach of the enemy, and now only a dozen coastwatchers and a handful of missionaries remained. There would be one less coastwatcher, Jessop reminded himself, if they should run into any Japanese patrol tonight.

In front of him Benny had stopped. 'No more path,' he explained, glancing over his shoulder. 'Go along bush this time.'

Jessop almost groaned aloud. The so-called track had been almost impenetrable, now he was to be denied even that solace. He hunched his shoulders and plunged after the youth. He could hear Senda padding tirelessly behind him but he did not look back at her.

The next thirty minutes were among the most excruciating of Jessop's life. Benny did his best to clear a path but he could not prevent the branches and creepers slashing the district officer's face and clawing at his legs. Jessop stumbled forward blindly, determined that he would not be the first to call a halt. The vague outline of trees whirled before his eyes in a crazy montage while the steady thrashing of Benny's bush knife blended with the buzzing of mosquitoes into a maddening accompaniment. Once he slipped and almost fell and it was Senda who held him. He rested on her for a moment and then dashed her arm aside, not meeting her gaze. He staggered on, close to total collapse. When Benny finally stopped the district officer stood swaying.

'How much farther?' he asked dazedly.

'No more. Him now.'

Jessop tried to focus his gaze. Ahead of them was a small natural clearing. Moonlight poured into it like a silver waterfall. Jessop could see a small makeshift hut. Two Solomon Islanders stood outside it, looking at him curiously. One of them clutched a piece of bone. Of course, thought Jessop, he would be the *velly* man. If other islanders knew that there was a magic man in the area they would avoid the hut. Putting his shoulders back Jessop walked towards the two Melanesians.

'Which way now,' he greeted them. 'Onefella 'Merican thisplace?'

'True now,' nodded the *velly* man. He indicated the hut. 'Himi sleep.'

Jessop nodded, trying not to reveal his exhaustion. He gestured to the others to stay where they were and went into the hut. A man was asleep on a woven mat in one corner of the room. He was very still. Jessop leant over the American pilot. What he saw caused him to recoil in surprise. The pilot was a coloured man.

4

There were so many layers of darkness that it was like being drawn along an endless tunnel. At first the shade was an all-pervading black but slowly it eased through a red-flecked spectrum to a ragged yellow. McKinley opened his eyes. He stared blankly at the roof, wondering where he was. Then rememberance came flooding in. He was back jockeying the single-seater Seagull along the coast, praying that the faltering engine would hold together long enough to enable him to make it back to Guadalcanal. Then there had been the final bowel-loosening lurch and the dizzy spectacle of the shore-line spiralling towards him as he fought to bring the aircraft down on the narrow expanse of level ground visible between the sea and the trees. After that there was nothing but a series of disjointed memories: of a ring of grave brown faces staring down at him, of being transported in a canoe, and then an interminable journey through trees and over uneven ground on some sort of litter.

'McKinley,' he muttered, 'you've come a long way to no evident purpose.'

He tried to sit up but flopped back as a shaft of pain throbbed through his head. Gingerly he eased his hands over his body. He seemed to have enough bruises to qualify for Joe Louis's bum-of-the-month club but as far as he could tell nothing was broken. That was just as well, he thought, considering that he seemed to have been sleeping on nothing but a couple of mats.

There was a sudden stir outside the hut and then a figure came in through the hole in the wall that served as a door. McKinley contemplated the newcomer without enthusiasm. He was young and thin, clad in white shorts and a shirt.

'Sanders of the River, I presume?' murmured the American.

'What?' The young man looked blank and then gave a perfunctory laugh. 'Oh, I see. No, my name's Jessop, Chris Jessop. I used to be the district officer in this part of the world, now I'm a coastwatcher for my sins.'

'Hi. I'm Dave McKinley.'

'McKinley?'

'Something wrong with that?'

'No, no, of course not. It was just the name. McKinley — it's Scottish, you see.'

'And I'm a nigra?'

Jessop went red. 'I'm sorry, I didn't mean — .'

'That's all right.' McKinley closed his eyes. 'Just like Johnny Dundee.'

'I beg your pardon? I'm afraid I don't quite — '

McKinley opened his eyes. 'Johnny Dundee,' he explained patiently. 'He used to be the world feather-weight champ. He was an Italian but he called himself Johnny Dundee. So he was known as the Scoth Wop.'

'I see,' said Jessop cautiously. 'Look, are you feeling all right now? I mean you haven't got concussion or anything?'

'Don't worry, I've still got all my marbles, Mr Jessop. I always talk like this. How's my chariot, by the way? A mite crumpled, I daresay.'

'Your aeroplane? I'm afraid I don't know. I should imagine the Japs have found it by now. I hope you can walk, McKinley. I want to get you away from here before any of their patrols get this far.'

'Where am I?'

'Halfway up a mountain in the middle of Renbanga. It's first light now. If you don't mind I'd like to get away as soon as possible.'

'I'll walk,' promised the pilot. 'I don't plan to spend the rest of the war in a p.o.w. camp.'

'Oh, I doubt if you'd do that,' said Jessop seriously. 'They wouldn't have any facilities for keeping prisoners down here. They'd probably interrogate you and then hang you from the nearest tree.'

'Thank you and good night.'

'Cheer up, it may never happen.'

'I intend to see that is doesn't.' McKinley gritted his teeth and began to haul himself to his feet. His body screamed in protest but eventually he succeeded in standing upright.

'All right,' he said. 'Where next?'

'We're going to walk round the mountain and then go down the other side. Then we'll get a canoe and I'll take you back to a small island where I spent most of my time. After that we'll make arrangements to get you back to your squadron.'

'Is that a fact? Just what are the odds on our making it?'

'I wouldn't know. I'm not a betting man.'

Pardon me for breathing, thought McKinley sourly. Man, we're going to have a barrel of laughs together. He hitched up his trousers and shuffled towards the door and then out into the clearing. Two Melanesians were waiting for him in the half-light of the rising sun, an adolescent youth grinning ingratiatingly and a girl so pretty that McKinley had difficulty in taking his eyes off her.

'Meet Benny and Senda,' said Jessop briefly, appearing at McKinley's shoulder. 'This is Mr McKinley.'

'Call me Mac,' said the American

68

automatically. 'Say, how long have you all been here?'

'About six hours. We got some sleep after we arrived. If you go through that gap in the trees over there, McKinley, you'll find a stream where you can wash. We'll start as soon as you get back.'

The American moved off in the direction indicated by the district officer. He brushed through the undergrowth and found a trickle of water coursing over the ground. As he knelt and laved his face and the back of his neck the pilot wondered what sort of a set-up he had encountered. The Englishman seemed to know what he was doing but he was as taut as a watch spring, anyone could see that. The girl was pretty though, really pretty. McKinley shook his head; he would have to play things by ear, he decided.

When he got back to the clearing the others were waiting for him. The sun was higher in the sky but the morning was still cool and fresh. Birds were singing in the trees. A third Melanesian had appeared and was talking to Jessop. The latter looked up as McKinley drew near.

'All right then,' he said. 'Let's go.'

'Just a minute,' replied McKinley absently. He looked at the man who had been talking to Jessop, recognition dawning. 'Isn't he one of the guys who carried me up here?'

'That's right,' nodded Jessop. 'His name's Mano. He's a village headman. He and Isaiah got you out of the 'plane and brought you up here. I've just been telling him that he's done a good job. I may even put him in for an official commendation.'

'That's nice,' commented McKinley drily. 'It'll be hard to top that.' He fumbled at his wrist and pulled off his watch. 'Here,' he said, offering it to Mano. 'I want you to have this. I owe you a lot.'

The headman took the watch, an expression of incredulous delight spreading across his face. It vanished when Jessop snatched the watch back and returned it to McKinley.

'Hey — ' protested the pilot.

'If the Japanese catch him with that

watch they'll know he's been in contact with you. They'll torture him until he tells them what he knows.'

'He can hide it — '

'I won't take that chance.'

McKinley glowered at the rigid district officer. 'You're what would be termed a stickler for detail, aren't you? Do you dress for dinner every night too?'

'I'm responsible for the lives of everyone in this party. Kindly allow me to know what's best for us all.'

'Yes, *sir*,' growled McKinley disgustedly. He turned to the crestfallen Melanesian. 'Sorry, buddy, you've just lost yourself a timepiece.'

'It's better than having red-hot splinters pushed under his finger-nails. If you're quite ready I'd like to start. I want to get down to the coast by dusk.'

'Lead on,' said McKinley. 'I'm in your hands, coastwatcher.'

★　★　★

Their progress down to the coast on the far side of Renbanga was not as rigorous

71

as the previous night's haul had been. In the light of day Benny was able to utilize a number of tracks. Once they had reached the far side of the mountain their route lay downhill. The densely packed trees kept off the worst of the heat. Even so, both McKinley and Jessop were glad to rest every two hours. At most halts Benny would climb a tree and provide them all with coconuts. Once Jessop produced a lump of yellow substance which he offered to the American.

'What's this?' asked McKinley.

'Sweet potato. Try some. You can almost get to like it.'

'Say after a hundred years. No thanks.'

'Suit yourself,' said Jessop equably, biting a chunk from the vegetable and chewing it. The district officer seemed to be in better spirits than at the start of the journey. McKinley hoped that this was a sign that things were going well.

'You've got a tough job,' ventured the pilot.

'It can be a bit of a strain sometimes,' admitted Jessop. 'I like the place and the people though. That helps. It's not knowing what's going on that's the worst. We don't get much news down in this part of the islands.'

'I can believe that.' McKinley tried to dredge up what few facts he could remember from the latest news bulletins. 'Things aren't too good,' he confessed. 'Rommel's advancing in North Africa and the Russians are taking a beating at Stalingrad. Oh yes, and the Japs seem to bc doing fine in New Guinea. That's about all, I guess.'

'You're right. Things aren't good. Still, they'll get better.'

'You're an optimist.'

Jessop looked hard at McKinley. 'I have to be,' he said eventually. He stood up. 'Come on, it's time we were moving.'

* * *

By four o'clock that afternoon they were within sight of the sea. An hour later they had stopped in a group among the trees just outside a coastal village.

'Benny says this is his home,' explained Jessop. 'He's going on ahead to make sure

73

that there aren't any Japs about.'

'Tell him he can be thorough,' said McKinley. 'I'm not in that much of a hurry.'

'With any luck you'll be flying again inside a week,' Jessop told him.

McKinley looked at the village. He had been on Guadalcanal for two months but when he had not been flying had hardly left the base. This was the first time he had seen a village close to. It was quite attractive, he decided with surprise. A few neat rows of bamboo huts with thatched roofs stood a hundred yards from the beach. Men and women were either sleeping in the sun or moving about unhurriedly. Children played noisily in the dust among the questing hens and dogs. There surely were less pleasant ways of living, thought the American.

Benny was gone for about fifteen minutes. When he returned across the sand his feet were dragging and his customary smile was missing. Jessop moved forward to meet the youth and they talked in undertones. Finally the district officer came back to McKinley and Senda.

'I can't quite make it out,' he said slowly. 'Benny says that it's all right for us to stay in the village until nightfall. The people here will lend us a canoe to take us round the island back to my village.'

'What's wrong with that?'

'I don't know,' frowned Jessop. 'I've a feeling something might be wrong somewhere. Benny swears that everything's fine, but he's looking pretty miserable.'

'What do you think then?'

Jessop mopped the sweat from his face with a tattered handkerchief. 'I think we can take a chance,' he said. 'It's only for a couple of hours. Anyway, all Solomon Islanders are loyal. It would hurt their feelings if we showed that we didn't trust them.'

'To hell with their frigging feelings,' declared McKinley vehemently. 'It's my neck I'm concerned about.'

'There are other considerations,' said Jessop coldly. 'As far as these people are concerned I represent the administration. If I insult them by refusing their hospitality they'll regard it as an official slight. Don't worry, it'll be all right.'

Jessop thrust his handkerchief back into his pocket and led the way across the intervening open ground to the village. At the sight of the little party men and women began to flock from their huts to form a chattering throng at the edge of the huts. They stood aside to allow one man to come forward. He was short and fat, wearing a faded pair of khaki shorts which clung affectionately to his ample belly. Faint tribal tattoo marks were etched across his cheeks. For all his apparent affability there was a seedy and raffish air to the man.

'Good-afternoon, Master Jessop,' he wheezed aimiably. 'Me lookim long you.'

'Voli,' said Jessop reflectively. 'Me forgettim you headman bilong this place.'

Voli grinned to reveal teeth and gums stained red by betel nut. 'Me happy too much for catchem D.O.,' he said unctuously.

'I bet,' said Jessop under his breath. Aloud he asked, 'Mebbe you catchem one place bilong mefella short time now?'

'True now, master. Onefella house bilong you close up ia.'

Voli turned and bustled ahead self-importantly like a grotesque parody of a head waiter, cleaving a way through the inquisitive crowd. Jessop gestured to his companions to follow him and then set off after the village headman. As they moved in the direction of a hut set away from the others at the far end of the village McKinley wondered at the air of constraint noticeable in the encounter between Jessop and Voli. The American's senses were further alerted when he saw Jessop muttering urgently to Senda and the girl nodding impassively in reply. It occurred to the pilot that he had not heard Senda speak once all day.

Before McKinley could move closer to Jessop and find out what was going on a small hand was suddenly thrust into one of his. A moment later he felt another hand thrust into his free hand. He looked down in surprise. A Melanesian child was attached to him on either side. The adults around him were smiling and nodding enthusiastically, calling out to the pilot.

Jessop glanced round at the noise and gave a tired smile.

'They've taken to you,' he said. 'You're the first black man they've seen wearing a white man's uniform.'

McKinley opened his mouth to reply but the headman had reached the hut and was pointing proudly at it.

'House bilong you, master,' he announced expansively. 'You sleep short time. Me catchem onefella canoe, come back time sun himi go.'

'Thank you, Voli,' acknowledged the district officer. 'Me wannem story long you little bit mebbe one hour. You savvy?'

'Me savvy good, Master Jessop, sir,' beamed the headman.

Under the benevolent gaze of most of the inhabitants of the village Jessop and McKinley entered the hut. The solitary room was dusty and neglected-looking. It contained no furniture except a few sacks upon which Jessop sank with a sigh of relief and began to remove one of his boots.

'Where are the others?' asked McKinley.

'Senda's gone off with the women. Benny should be with his parents.' Jessop took off a sock and examined his foot dolefully. 'If you're feeling lonely just take a look outside the door.'

McKinley walked back to the piece of sacking covering the entrance and peered out. Over a hundred men, women and chilren were sitting expectantly on the ground in serried ranks. The sun shone on their glistening brown bodies. When they saw McKinley they broke into a spontaneous burst of applause.

'They clapped me, for Christ's sake,' said a stupefied McKinley, dropping the sacking and returning to the cool gloom of the room.

'Go back and take a bow,' suggested Jessop. 'Very good for international relations, this sort of thing. You might be able to make a permanent job out of it.'

'No thanks,' said McKinley, subsiding on to the floor. 'I've got enough problems as it is.'

The door covering was brushed aside again and two women came in carrying coconuts and a pawpaw which they put on the floor between the two men. When they had withdrawn McKinley spoke again.

'You didn't seem too pleased to see that headman,' he suggested.

'Voli? No, he's the one man I would have chosen not to meet. He's an engaging old rogue but definitely not to be trusted. He's got the gift of the gab though. Years ago he conned the Melanesian Mission into sending him to Australia to train for the ministry.'

'And he was a dismal failure?'

'Not dismal — spectacular. He ran up debts, got women into trouble, damn nearly caused an international incident. The Mission had to bring him back double-quick time. Since then he's been a school-teacher, gold-miner and I don't know what. We had to make him headman because he's the only educated islander around these parts.'

'Do you know everybody around here then?' asked McKinley.

'No, of course not,' said Jessop, putting his sock back on and lacing up his boot.

'But I like to know what's going on in my district.'

'Your district?' queried McKinley, raising an eyebrow. 'Seems to me this patch of ground belongs to Emperor Hirohito just now.'

'Strictly a temporary situation. This is British territory. When we kick the Japs out a great deal of reconstruction is going to be needed. That's why I'm keeping an eye on things.'

'I saw a fellow like you once before,' marvelled the pilot. 'It was at the movies. The George Sanders character in *The Sun Never Sets*.'

'If I keep at it I may graduate to C. Aubrey Smith,' Jessop told him. 'This is all a joke to you, isn't it?'

'Well . . . ' McKinley spread his hands. 'I don't go overboard for the salute the flag, hail to Old Glory razamataz. That's one thing.'

'And the other?'

McKinley looked levelly at the Englishman. 'The other?' he drawled silkily. 'Seeing that you ask, I don't like to see a handful of white men pushing a hundred thousand blacks around.'

'I see,' said Jessop calmly. 'I thought it might be something like that. Well you're wrong. This isn't the U.S.A. We treat coloured people properly here.'

'Oh sure. A pat on the head and a bone for a good dog. They tell me it's called paternalism.'

'You haven't been here long enough to know anything about it. And in any case, whatever goes on in the Solomons is none of your business.'

'Is that so? You Limeys needed us to get you out of trouble on Guadalcanal. I don't see any Limey soldiers fighting there.'

'If you had been here longer than five minutes,' said Jessop, ignoring the last jibe, 'you'd know that if it wasn't for the British administration this place would be back in the Stone Age. There may not be all that much here yet, but what there is has been brought here by the missionaries and the British.'

'Sure,' sneered McKinley. 'Rule Britannia, Land of Hope and Glory. You'll pardon me if I don't stand up and sing three verses of *God Save the King*. No dice. As far as I'm concerned the Solomons are just another stinking little red dot on the map.'

'Tell me,' asked Jessop icily. 'Are you anti-white or just anti-British?'

'Both, man. I'm completely impartial in my prejudices.'

'Obviously. Then all I can say is that you're a disgrace to both your uniform and your race.'

McKinley scrambled to his feet, an ugly look on his face. 'How would you like a sock on the nose?' he demanded, advancing on Jessop.

The Englishman stood up quickly. Reaching to one side he tore a bamboo support from the wall and lifted it. The two men circled each other. Before either of them could move forward the door-covering swung aside and Senda hurried into the hut. She seized Jessop's arm and drew him to one side, whispering into his ear while McKinley watched sullenly.

'What is this?' he asked.

Jessop dropped his bamboo pole. 'Bad

news, I'm afraid,' he answered briefly. 'I was afraid of this. Senda says she's just seen Benny out in the bush. He's bringing a patrol of Japanese soldiers back with him.'

5

'Japanese!' echoed McKinley. 'What the hell are we going to do?'

'Get away if we can,' said Jessop, who was very pale. 'How far off are they, Senda?'

'About twenty minutes' walk. I saw them coming down the mountains.'

'What is this?' exploded a bewildered McKinley. 'You act as if you were expecting it.'

'I thought there was a chance,' said Jessop in an undertone, almost talking to himself, 'but it had to be taken.' He fell silent and turned away from the others.

'Mr Jessop knew that Benny was Voli's nephew and would have to do as the headman told him,' explained Senda quickly, her compassionate eyes on the district officer. 'He asked me to follow Voli and Benny. A patrol had left the village just before we arrived. Voli knew he could catch up with it. Benny didn't want to go but he belongs to Voli's line. He had no choice.'

'Poor Benny,' said Jessop simply. He glanced shyly at McKinley as if appealing for understanding. 'In a way these are my people. I had to go along with them.'

'Now I know you're mad,' said the American bitterly. 'I'm telling you, man, you got me into this, you get me out.'

'We'll take to the bush again,' said Jessop. 'We won't have a local guide and Voli will turn the whole village out to help the Japs look for us, but it's about the only thing we can do.'

'There is another way,' said Senda.

The two men stared at her, they had almost forgotten the existence of the girl. Senda looked embarrassed but did not flinch.

'How?' asked Jessop gently.

'Manno,' answered the girl.

For a moment the district officer looked disconcerted. Then he shook his head vigorously. 'Out of the question,' he said. 'It's quite impossible.'

'It's not impossible. The people outside are saying it already. It all fits together, you see. The black man who comes down out of the sky and walks with white men as an equal.'

'Is somebody going to let me in on this?' asked McKinley loudly.

'It's nothing,' said Jessop brusquely. 'Just some crazy idea of Senda's that would never work. There's no time to discuss it now. We've got to get out of this village.'

'If we go back into the bush,' said Senda matter-of-factly, 'we'll be caught and killed in an hour. If we are to stay alive we must persuade the people of this village to help us.'

Jessop paused in his progress to the door. He ran his sweating palms down the side of his shorts. The look that he gave Senda was one of annoyance.

'You know that I speak the truth,' the girl said softly.

'We'd never get away with it.'

'We might in this village — if you said it was so.'

'If what was so?' asked an exasperated McKinley. 'Will somebody kindly tell me what's going on?'

Jessop waved the negro aside and turned away, trying to think. It was Senda who answered McKinley's question.

'There is a custom — a tradition,' she said. 'Not many villages have it but some do. This is one of them. The story is that one day a black man will come down from the sky and unite all the islands and make the people rich. They call that man Manno.'

'And they think that I'm Manno?' gasped the American.

'Some of the people think that you might be. They have heard that you fell from the sky yesterday and came straight to them. I think they would acclaim you if you went out and said that you were Manno — if Mr Jessop confirmed it.'

'Let me get this straight. If I said I was this guy Manno, would they help us escape from the Japs?'

'If they thought you were Manno they would do anything you asked.'

'Well come on then, what are we waiting for? If it meant getting out of this place in one piece I'd claim to be Two Ton Tony Galento.'

'It's not as easy as that,' said Jessop. 'There's a matter of principle involved. British administrators have spent thirty years building up a reputation for probity. These people believe what we tell them. Now you're asking me to tell them an outright lie.'

'For God's sake — !'

'It's the only way,' insisted Senda doggedly. 'If you tell them that Mac is Manno they will help you to escape. If you get away Mac will go back to Guadalcanal where they will never see him again. The people will think that he has gone back to his home in the skies.'

'She's right,' urged McKinley. 'One white lie and we're away. 'What can be wrong with that?'

'A great deal,' said Jessop unhappily, 'but I can see that there is no point in trying to make you understand. All the same I am responsible for the lives of all three of us, I appreciate that.' He fell silent, chewing his lip. When he looked up his expression was grim. 'Very well, we'll give it a try.'

'Now you're talking,' applauded the

American. 'Let's go out there and make with the words.'

'No, you two wait in here. I'll go out and prepare them.'

'Suit yourself, but do me a favour — hurry it up, will you? We don't have too much time left.'

'I'll be as quick as I can,' said Jessop, and went out.

McKinley and Senda stood listening in the dusty room. They heard a rising babble of noise as Jessop appeared and then it died away as the district officer began to address the assembled villagers. McKinley tried to ignore the shaking of his knees; he had never been so frightened.

'It's mad,' he said, shaking his head. 'This Manno business. What does it make me — some sort of a god to a bunch of natives?'

'It's not so unusual. Many societies have a tradition of a Messiah expected from the skies. Even in your America, I think.'

'Sorry,' said the negro contritely. 'I'm so scared I'm just shooting off at the mouth.' He ran a hand over his face. 'It's been a rough day, put it down to that.' He smiled at Senda. 'My guess is that you're a school-teacher.'

'What makes you think that?'

'The way you speak English and the fact that you knew about the Messiah tradition.'

'We're not all savages swinging from the trees.'

'I've said I'm sorry. All right, I'll go farther. I'll give you a choice. Do you want me to cut my throat or shoot myself? How's that for an offer?'

In spite of herself the girl giggled. 'I don't want you to do either.' She collected herself. 'Have you always flown aeroplanes?'

'No, I used to be a sports writer. Mostly I covered the fights. Not the big ones at the Garden, but I worked St Nick's Arena now and again as well as the smaller places. A lot of fighters are coloured, see, so they used me for digging out background material as well as doing reports.'

Senda looked bemused. 'Mac,' she said

hesitantly, 'I think I did not understand you at all then.'

'Don't let it bother you, kid. I'm just talking to keep my mind off what's happening.'

A roar of approbation from the people outside made them both swing round to face the door. Involuntarily Senda put a hand on McKinley's arm. After a few seconds Jessop came into the room, sweat dripping from his face.

'All right,' he panted. 'I've set them up. Now it's your turn, McKinley.'

The negro nodded nervously. 'With you,' he said. He did not move.

Jessop stood pointedly to one side. Slowly McKinley walked past him into the sunshine of the late afternoon. A frenzy of cheers greeted him. The pilot blinked in amazement. The crowd had swelled until there were more than two hundred men and women before him. They were all on their feet, screaming enthusiastically. In spite of his app-rehension McKinley experienced an unexpected surge of elation and power. As the villagers waved and shouted he slowly raised both arms to their full extent above his head in an all-embracing gesture. As the noise of the crowd became deafening he let out a stentorian roar.

'I am Manno!' he cried.

★ ★ ★

This time they were making their way through the jungle at the foot of the mountain, parallel with the sea. It was almost six o'clock in the evening and the sun was going down. There were twelve men escorting them. Ten more had gone up into the mountain and a further dozen had scattered in all directions among the trees and undergrowth. With so many false trails being laid Voli would never be able to track them down on his own. The rest of the villagers had been enjoined to plead ignorance when the Japanese patrol turned up.

The headman would go berserk when he discovered what had happened, thought McKinley with satisfaction. The American was still slightly dazed by events. He had only a vague recollection of the tumultuous acclamation coming from the villagers and of Jessop stepping in to issue his instructions. Now, according to the district officer, they were approaching the next village along the coast, where a canoe would be waiting for them.

The trees were thinning and ahead of them McKinley saw the huts of a village almost identical with the one they had left behind them. He could hear a muffled sound which at first he took to be the pounding of the surf on a reef, but then he saw the men and women running towards him in their hundreds and he knew that it was their voices that he had heard.

'Hell's bells,' swore Jessop. 'The word's got ahead.' He moved quickly into action, shouting orders to the escort. Hastily the men joined arms and ran forward to form a human barrier between McKinley and the villagers. At first it looked as if the guards would be swept aside but the men dug their heels into the ground and clung grimly to each other. Behind them Jessop shouted hoarsely in pidgin at the clamouring men and women. At first they ignored him but slowly his words percolated and the noise died away as they waited expectantly.

'You'll have to say something,' muttered the distant officer, coming back to the pilot. 'I've promised them you'd speak to them. I've never seen anything like this. You've really woken 'em up.'

'What shall I say?' asked McKinley.

'Search me. You're their god, I'm not.'

'You're a great help,' grunted the American. 'Reckon I better give them my theme song.'

'Give them something anyway.'

The American stepped forward and raised a hand. 'Manno!' he cried, and again 'Manno!'.

The shout of response that went up from the assembled Solomon Islanders was almost frightening in its intensity. The noise was harsh and full-throated like the baying of an enormous hound. Standing in the background Jessop surveyed the faces of the possessed throng. He had never seen Melanesians so animated.

The front rank of the crowd was being heaved forward in a gigantic wave by those behind. Hands stretched out to touch McKinley. The men guarding him were being pushed back, step by straining step. Jessop was worried. He wondered what dark forces had been unleashed in the normally placid villagers. This mass hysteria could easily spread and give rise to all sorts of problems. The sooner McKinley was hustled out of the district the better it would be for everyone. In the meantime there was the present turmoil to be controlled.

There was no doubt that the situation was getting out of hand. The ten men protecting the American had been forced back a dozen paces. Several had been forced apart and one had fallen to his knees. McKinley fought to keep his footing. Around him the adoring, shining faces were thrust close to his. Dozens of hands clutched at him and tore his clothing. The peculiar musk-like odour of too many bodies hung like a cloud. Panic began to seize the pilot. What a way to go, he thought dully, torn to pieces by a pack of would-be disciples.

Suddenly the pressure eased. Hands stopped clawing at him. The noise died away until the silence was as oppressive as any din. The Melanesians closest to the pilot began to shuffle back. Some of them squeezed to one side, forming an avenue through the crowd. McKinley saw a man walking down the avenue towards him. He was moving slowly with the deliberation of extreme old age. When the old man was closer McKinley could see that his eyes were blank and sightless.

'Who's this?' demanded the American, looking desperately over his shoulder at Jessop. 'What does he want?'

The district officer shook his head helplessly. 'I don't know,' he said. 'He's not the headman. Those I do know.'

McKinley snarled something obscene and turned back. The blind man had stopped some six feet away. His emaciated brown body, clad only in a tattered loin-cloth, was scarred and tattoo-marked. The empty staring sockets dominated a wizened and pitted face. One of the men in the crowd came forward and led the blind man closer to McKinley.

'Which way now?' demanded Jessop loudly.

A grey-haired Melanesian spoke quietly to the district officer. Jessop listened attentively until the man had finished and then thanked him courteously.

'The blind man spent five years in Queensland as an indentured labourer fifty years ago,' he whispered, putting his mouth close to the American's ear. 'There aren't many of them around any more. He's the only man in these parts who's lived among white men. That's why the people have brought him here now. He's a big man in their eyes. They think he'll be able to tell if you're really Manno or not.'

'The hell he will,' muttered McKinley. 'Suppose he says I'm not.'

Jessop cast a practised eye at the crowd. The former wild enthusiasm had given way to a simmering controlled energy which was both impressive and alarming.

'If they take it into their heads that we've been fooling them,' replied the

Englishman tersely, 'they'll tear us to pieces.'

'Great,' said McKinley, his lips tightening.

Jessop shrugged. 'You're on your own, I'm afraid,' he told the other man. 'They won't listen to me any more.'

Abruptly the negro moved forward until he was standing directly in front of the blind man. The crowd sighed softly. The blind man extended his hands and clutched McKinley's arms. Then he slid his grasp up until he was holding the pilot's shoulders. He stood quite still for twenty seconds. Finally he placed his hands on McKinley's face.

The American tried not to flinch as the rough fingers explored his features. After a few moments the blind man dropped his hands heavily to his sides and stepped back, nodding slightly. He opened his toothless mouth and emitted a high-pitched cackle.

'Manno!' he crowed.

McKinley was conscious of an overwhelming sensation of relief. Before he could give way to it the crowd broke its ranks, screaming, and began to charge towards him. Automatically he gave a warning cry. The leaders of the mob hesitated. McKinley filled his lungs and shouted again with all his force. Puzzled, the crowd fell back slightly. The American seized Jessop by the elbow.

'Quick, man,' he hissed. 'Tell 'em I'm a god and mustn't be touched. Otherwise we'll be swamped.'

The district officer looked startled but recovered quickly. 'No more!' he yelled, pushing in front of the negro. 'Tambu! Tambu!'

'Tambu.' The word was taken up by the villagers and passed among them respectfully. After some deliberation they fell back further, making a path for McKinley and the others.

'I don't know what tambu means, but it seems to work,' slurred McKinley out of the corner of his mouth as he and the Englishman walked between the rows of Melanesians with Senda following.

'It's the local variation on *tabu* — forbidden,' explained Jessop in an

100

undertone. 'From now on that's you, McKinley.'

The American raised his eyebrows but did not answer. The sun was low in the sky and the trees were casting long shadows on the sand. McKinley could see some of the younger men running ahead. They stopped at an open-ended shelter on the beach and went inside. A few moments later they reappeared. This time they were sliding a large, ornately decorated canoe towards the sea. The craft bore an impressive figurehead and the sides were richly carved.

'The war canoe,' observed Jessop. 'They're really giving you an impressive send-off. They don't bring it out more than once a year as a rule.'

'It looks big enough.'

'It had to be. Canoes like that used to pick up slaves from Isabel a hundred years ago. Now it looks as if it's going to take us home.'

When they reached the beach the canoe was in the water with a dozen oarsmen already on board waiting for them. The rest of the villagers gathered on the beach. McKinley stopped, wondering whether he ought to say something, but an almost imperceptible shake of the head from Jessop dissuaded him and he contented himself with lifting an arm in farewell.

As he did so he took in the picture. The crowd was drawn up in a semi-circle on the sand. The canoe, beautiful in its flamboyant savagery of another age, bobbed gently on the waves. The sun was setting below the horizon, casting a delicate scarlet web over the sea. McKinley thought it was one of the loveliest sights he had ever witnessed.

'It'll be dark in ten minutes,' said Jessop practically. 'It's safe enough to start now.'

'What about Japanese ships?'

Jessop shook his head. 'They can't cover every inch of the coast. Anyway, we'll be able to stay close to the shore *and* still go at a rate of knots with twelve men to row us. We should be all right.'

McKinley followed Jessop and Senda into the water. Before he could reach the canoe a small boy had darted out from the crowd in a last effort to touch the American. Missing his footing he stumbled and fell in the shallow water. McKinley stooped and picked the child up, handing him back to one of the women. Jessop called urgently from the canoe and the American waded out to the vessel and climbed on board. An old man sitting in the stern hit a makeshift drum. The men dipped their oars into the water and as the old man beat time they rowed out towards the sunset.

McKinley sat in the centre of the canoe with Jessop and Senda. Once he turned and waved to the villagers on the beach. Their arms rose in reply like a many-headed snake. The American turned to Senda.

'Something I've been meaning to ask you,' he said. 'This name Manno — what does it mean?'

'In the language of these people it means the Lord of Life,' answered the girl.

'It does?' McKinley savoured the expression. 'The Lord of Life, eh? Well there's a thing.'

6

'Remember, we only want one of the bastards,' warned Bannion. 'Any more and we'll cut their throats.'

Sam Thomas grunted. The two men were lying behind a cassava bush at the edge of the undergrowth a little to one side of a trail leading to a water hole. They had been waiting there most of the morning. On several occasions Japanese soldiers had come down to the stream to wash, but each time there had been at least three of them, and Bannion and Thomas had been forced to restrain themselves. The Australian was growing impatient.

'Dirty buggers,' he grumbled. 'Don't any of 'em take a bath?'

'Here's one,' said Thomas suddenly.

Cautiously Bannion raised his head. The half-caste was right. Someone was coming along the trail, whistling. After a few seconds a Japanese soldier sauntered round the bend. The man was middle-aged and bespectacled, wearing the unkempt uniform of a private. This one would not be much trouble, decided Bannion. Many of the troops on this part of Renbanga were in holding companies and were not highly trained soldiers. The man they were watching now looked more like a clerk than a rifleman. Which was just as well, reflected the Australian. Tulagi had asked for a Japanese prisoner, and an office worker should know more than some foot-slogger. This one came from a small company of pioneers building a pill-box a hundred yards away. Bannion had borne the place in mind for some time and was now moving in.

'He's going off the track,' warned Thomas.

'What?' Bannion hoisted himself up again in time to see the soldier turning off into the bush, loosening his belt as he did so. 'Like that, is it? All right, sport, it looks like we're going to catch you with your pants down.'

Bannion and Thomas waited another five minutes in order to make sure that the Japanese was alone. Then, at a signal from the Australian, the two men rose, clutching their sten guns, and hurried down to the track. They reached it and tiptoed into the undergrowth on the other side in the direction taken by the soldier. They paused for a moment. Thomas hardly needed the signal from Bannion to send him circling round to come in behind their quarry. The Australian allowed his companion a minute in which to disappear among the trees and then went forward on his own.

He found the Japanese squatting at the foot of a tree. The soldier's trousers were down about his ankles and his rifle was propped against the trunk of the tree. When he saw Bannion an expression compounded of astonishment and shame contorted his face. Frantically he rocked to one side on his haunches, scrabbling to reach his rifle. Thomas stepped out from behind the tree and secured the weapon.

'It just isn't your day,' Bannion told the Japanese. 'Pull up your trousers and let's go.'

The soldier hauled up his trousers and

fastened his belt with trembling hands. He did not look at his captors. When he was ready he stood sagging before them. Bannion could smell the acrid aroma of fear on the little man.

'I don't think he's going to make a noise,' remarked the Australian. 'All the same — '

Thomas nodded and stepped in behind the Japanese. Reversing his sten gun he drove the butt brutally into the nape of the little man's neck. The latter crumpled and fell. While Thomas threw him over his massive shoulder in a fireman's lift Bannion stooped and picked up the soldier's rifle. Removing the bolt he hurled it into the bush before throwing the rifle in the other direction. Then the two men hurried away with their prisoner.

It took them half an hour to make their way through the bush to the inlet where the *Nancy* was anchored. Although their journey was made in the full heat of the day Thomas's pace did not slacken. They came out of the trees at the double and raced down the shingle to the edge of the water. The schooner swung at anchor thirty yards off the shore. At the sight of the two men three Melanesians jumped from the deck down into the dinghy tied to the rail. Casting off the rope they began to pull hurriedly for the shore.

As they waited for the rowing-boat to reach them Thomas absently lowered the Japanese to the ground. The man groaned feebly and began to retch at their feet. Bannion and Thomas paid little attention to him. Their eyes were on the dinghy which, for all the efforts of its crew, seemed to be approaching with agonizing slowness. Bannion had chosen this particular inlet deliberately for its position. Among the thousands of similar mangrove-covered indentations off the coast the anchorage was indistinguishable from its neighbours. It was extremely unlikely that a Japanese vessel or aircraft would stumble across the bay except by accident, but the chance was always there. In that harbour the *Nancy* would be helpless against any attack. Neither Bannion nor Thomas would be happy until they were secure among the anonymity of the thousands of square miles of sea surrounding the Solomons.

The Japanese soldier hauled himself to his knees like a boxer beaten insensible but coming back into the fight on spirit alone. The others eyed him tolerantly as he staggered to his feet and lurched into the water. He stood irresolutely for a second and then flopped forward on to his face in the shallows.

'He's really in a bad way,' commented Bannion idly, watching the bubbles rising around the soldier's recumbent form. 'Seems to me we ought — ' He stopped, realisation dawning. 'Get him!' he yelled, darting forward. 'He's trying to drown himself!'

They reached the Japanese together and dragged him upright. The little man was coughing harshly and inhaling between bouts with great shuddering breaths. Bannion shook him fiercely.

'You bloody ratbag!' he yelled, white with rage. 'I ought to crease you!'

'Mr Bannion.' The Australian felt Thomas's hand on his shoulder. Looking up sharply he saw the big man indicating the dinghy which had reached the beach, its crew members watching the scene with interest.

Reluctantly Bannion released the Japanese, pushing him away. 'Take him away before I kill him,' he grated. 'Get him on board.'

Thomas propelled the semi-conscious soldier ahead of him on to the dinghy and helped the Melanesians push it out into deep water before jumping on board with them. The crew took up their oars as Bannion climbed into the boat, and started pulling for the schooner. Throughout the journey the Australian sat lowering at the solider shivering in the bottom of the dinghy.

No one said anything until they were on board the *Nancy*. The dinghy was secured to the side of the vessel and Bannion went to the wheel, issuing curt orders to one of the Melanesians, who hurried down into the engine-room. Thomas, keeping one hand on the shoulder of the Japanese, supervised the winching up of the anchor. The engines coughed to life and Bannion headed the vessel for the open sea.

When the coast was five miles behind him the Australian handed over the wheel to one of the Solomon Islanders.

'Keepim allsame thisfella, Henry,' he commanded, stepping back. He looked at Thomas and his prisoner. 'Take him down to the hold and lock him in,' he said. 'Take his clothes off and make sure there's nothing in the hold he can use to damage himself. Have one of the boys on guard outside — and make sure he stays outside. Then report to me in the cabin.'

'Yes, sir,' nodded the half-caste. He eased the Japanese towards the companionway. 'Move off, soldier.'

* * *

Ten minutes later Thomas tapped at the door of the cabin. At a word from Bannion he went in. In the confined space the Australian was sitting on his bunk, a bottle of whisky and two empty glasses balanced at his side.

'Sit down, Sam,' he invited, indicating a canvas chair in a corner. 'Have a drink.' He filled the glasses and handed one to the half-caste. 'This is the last bottle. Everything all right below?'

'Everything's fine,' said the half-caste.

'Good.' Bannion sipped his drink and then stared reflectively into the glass. 'You thought I went too far on the beach, didn't you?'

'You lost your temper, boss, that's all.'

'That's right, I lost my temper.' Bannion's eyes lifted from the glass. 'I've been doing that a lot lately, Sam.'

Thomas cleared his throat in embarrassment. 'You've got a lot of worries,' he said. 'You're under a strain.'

'You reckon? Yeah, maybe you're right. But that doesn't alter the fact, does it? If I keep losing my temper my judgement will go and then we'll be in real trouble.' He swallowed his drink. 'What I'm trying to say is that I'm sorry I acted up ashore just now. I didn't mean to hurt that Jap. If it happens again you'd better kick me up the arse.'

'Sure, boss.' Thomas tried to lighten the atmosphere. 'If you're feeling like that, how about another glass of whisky while it lasts?'

Bannion did not rise to the bait. He filled both glasses. 'You know,' he said sombrely, 'before the war I'll swear I didn't have a care in the world. I was the life and soul of any bloody party. I sailed the *Nancy* round the islands and I always had enough in my pocket for a bottle and a woman. I didn't know when I was well off.' He leaned back disconsolately in his bunk. 'That Jap,' he said abruptly. 'What do you make of him?'

'Make of him?' asked the half-caste in surprise. 'I don't know, boss. He's a brave one.'

'He's that all right. Not many of us would try to drown ourselves like that. Makes you think, doesn't it? I mean, I always reckon the Japs to be a bunch of yellow bastards with nothing much to 'em. Then you meet one and you realise that you don't understand 'em at all.'

'I don't think about things like that, boss.'

'Then you're bloody lucky, mate.' Bannion sat up, dismissing the subject. 'All right, let's see if we've got things straight. We should reach Voli's village in

113

five hours. We'll drop you there and go on the Kukala. Right?'

'Right.'

'You're sure you don't want the *Nancy* to wait for you off Voli's place?'

Thomas shook his head. 'I'm sure. I want to get the feel of the place before I go in and get Benny.'

'And you're definite it's only Benny you want? You don't want to pick up that bastard Voli too?'

Again Thomas was definite. 'No, I don't. He's an old crook but he is a headman. If we take him away his people will try and stop us. It's not worth starting that amount of trouble for.'

'I suppose so,' said Bannion dubiously. 'It rubs me up to let the bastard get away with it though. We'll keep an eye on him. If I know Jessop he'll be on to Tulagi to get Voli chucked out of his job.'

'They were lucky to escape.'

'You can say that again. I wanted to talk to you about it. What have you heard about that caper?'

'Well ... ' said Thomas slowly. 'It's hard to tell the truth of it. The story is that Jessop and Senda turned up at the village with Manno, the promised one, and that Manno talked the villagers into helping them get away.'

'Manno,' scoffed the Australian. 'A Yank Seagull crashed on the coast the day before. It must have been the pilot Jessop had with him.' A note of reluctant admiration entered Bannion's voice. 'It was quick thinking though. I never reckoned Jessop to have it in him.'

'The story's spread,' remarked Thomas, watching the other man intently. 'It's all over the district now. Do you want me to pass the word that it's all rubbish?'

'No,' said Bannion decisively. He saw the surprise in Thomas's eyes and went on to explain. 'Not yet anyway. I want to see how things go. If this Manno things stirs the people up it could be a good thing.'

'I don't see how, boss.'

'Unity,' said Bannion. 'That's what they call it. You know what they're like in this district. Every village sticks to itself. You never get all the people united to do one thing. Maybe Manno can do

115

it. Let's wait and see.'

'I get it,' said the half-caste admiringly. 'You reckon Manno might persuade the people to get together to fight the Japs.'

'I don't know if Manno will,' said Bannion coolly. 'But if he turns out to be as influential as some think he will, we might be able to lean on him a little.'

* * *

Five hours later Thomas went ashore near Voli's village. He refused the services of the dinghy and swam the hundred yards to the shore. He was aware of eyes observing him from the undergrowth but gave no sign of it. Glancing back at the *Nancy* he saw that the schooner was already moving away. The half-caste brushed some of the water from his body. The fact that the vessel had not lingered should have reassured the onlookers. He started to walk up to the village.

There were no women or children about, which was significant. Men were standing outside each of the huts. Their hands were empty but Thomas knew that spears and fighting sticks would be piled inside the houses. The half-caste ignored the villagers; even though he had no high opinion of the warlike ability of the men from this part of the island he was not going to antagonize a hundred of them unless he had to.

He found Voli sitting in his hut. The chief was alone and no one attempted to prevent Thomas entering the hut but the half-caste heard the drift of footsteps as the men of the village gathered outside, and knew that he would not leave unless he had Voli's permission.

'Sit down, Sam,' invited the headman. 'You've come a long way.'

Thomas squatted on the floor and accepted the slice of pawpaw offered by the headman. The fact that Voli was speaking English and not pidgin was a sign that he was not going to waste time. Voli only used pidgin when addressing Government officers and missionaries. When he wanted to get down to business he used language or English.

'I've come for Benny,' announced the half-caste.

'Only him?'

Thomas nodded. 'You're lucky this time, Voli. Mr Bannion will punish Benny, not you.'

The headman looked indifferent but Thomas could tell from a slackening in the Melanesian's posture that the man was relieved.

'Benny is my line,' said Voli. 'I don't think I can let him go.'

'You'll let him go. Otherwise your village will suffer.'

'You're behind the times, man. The British don't send a gunboat to shoot our houses down any more. They did that fifty years ago in the Roviana Lagoon, but no more.'

'There are other ways.'

'What sort of ways?'

'They could take away your headman's allowance.'

'In the middle of a war? The British aren't that stupid. Jessop might like them to overthrow me, but he's a young man. I'm safe enough, Sam.'

You probably are, too, thought Thomas. Voli was a professional survivor. He was the sort of man who swayed comfortably in storms that would break stronger but less resilient people. Yet outside his own district he would never amount to anything. The man was too lazy and narrow-minded. He would not develop into the leader that the Solomons would need when the war was over, Thomas was convinced of that.

'But are you safe?' he asked, taking up Voli's point. 'What about Manno? Your own village turned against you over him.'

'A misunderstanding,' said Voli smoothly. 'Manno had not manifested himself properly when I first met him. It was not until I had left that he declared himself to be the Lord of Life.'

'After you'd left to fetch the Japanese.'

'What?' Voli's eyes widened. 'You're making a mistake, Sam. I didn't fetch the Japanese. No, no. I heard that Benny had gone to fetch the patrol and I ran after him to stop him, but it was too late.'

You cunning bastard, thought Thomas. Poor Benny will never be able to contradict you. It looks as if you've swum ashore again, Voli.

'And you are telling your people that the coloured man who came here with Jessop was Manno?' he asked.

'Of course,' said a poker-faced Voli. 'That's who he was. I feel honoured that it was my village that Manno chose to visit first. I have told my people that Manno intends me as one of his chief disciples. Why else would he have come here?'

Thomas could not restrain a pang of reluctant admiration. Voli was cunning enough. It looked as if he had talked himself out of a potentially dangerous situation. He had also considerably strengthened Manno's hand. What with Jessop and Voli backing him the man's credentials were growing all the time.

'What about you and Bannion?' asked Voli shrewdly. 'What do you say about Manno?'

'It's too early to tell yet,' was the half-caste's cautious reply. 'We want to see this Manno before we decide.'

'Very sensible,' nodded Voli, a gleam of appreciation in his eye. He rocked comfortably on his haunches, looking like a brown, badly carved replica of Buddha. 'I think we understand each other, Sam.'

'You're a clever man, Voli,' said Thomas sincerely.

'I'm a realist,' acknowledged the headman calmly. 'I am not like the Fijians and the missionary. Did you hear about them?'

Thomas shook his head and Voli took up the tale with the aplomb of a professional story-teller. While he spoke his eyes, small and button-hard, remained on Thomas.

'It happened many years ago,' began the headman, 'when the first European missionary arrived in Fiji. Naturally the people, being sensible men and women, killed and ate him. That was fine, but unfortunately the missionary had been wearing leather boots. Now the missionary had been very tasty, but the people just could not digest his boots. They tried all ways of preparing them. They boiled the boots and baked them and fried them but they could not make them eatable. That really worried the poor Fijians; they quite forgot how much they had enjoyed eating the missionary and only remembered how much misfortune they had had with his boots.' Voli smiled slightly and for once there was also a glint of amusement in his eyes. 'I would not be like those foolish Fijians, Sam. I might have eaten the missionary but I would not have wasted my time on his boots.'

'We understand each other,' said Thomas, standing up. 'Now I want to take Benny back to Kukala for his punishment.'

'Suppose I don't let him go?' asked Voli casually.

'Then you would have to kill me. If you did that Mr Bannion would come to this village with twenty Malaita men and burn it down and hang you by your testicles from the nearest tree. You know that is true. Mr Bannion is not British, he is Australian. Australians do not stick to the rules. They do what they think is right.'

'It is possible,' said Voli indifferently, and Thomas knew that his thrust had gone home as he had intended.

'However,' went on the headman indifferently, 'there is no problem. If you can find Benny you can take him back to Kukala. It is of course right that he should be punished.'

'I'll find him,' promised Thomas.

Voli allowed the half-caste to get as far as the door before he spoke. 'Sam,' he asked, 'why are you helping Bannion? It puzzles me. I would really like to know.'

'I'm not helping Bannion,' Thomas told him. 'I'm helping the British Government.'

'Why?'

'Because the British have been here for forty years. They were here before the Japanese came and they'll be here after the Japanese have left.'

'And the British will reward you for your loyalty? Very clever, Sam. But what happens if the Japanese win, have you thought of that?'

'I don't want to think about it,' said Thomas.

He went outside. The waiting men made way for him with an ill-grace. Their unconcealed hostility surprised Thomas. Something unusual must have happened to have stirred up these normally docile folk. It was not likely to have been Voli's influence so it must have been the appearance of the stranger calling himself Manno.

Thomas looked round, wondering where Benny was hiding. If the villagers were going to refuse to cooperate there was no point in searching aimlessly. The half-caste decided to go back to the beach and wait.

He sat among the canoes and fishing-nets, staring out at the reef. As he waited he wondered what reply he would have given to Voli's question if he had been honest. He certainly was not helping the British for the reason suggested by the headman. Thomas had no feelings one way or the other for the British administration. He accepted it as he accepted tides and the seasons. He was not risking his life assisting the coast-watcher for the hope of any reward. It was difficult to put into words the reason for his action. Thomas only knew that when the war ended there would be changes and that he thought the British would be more amenable to them than the Japanese would be.

Thomas had been waiting on the beach for half an hour when Benny finally appeared, as the half-caste had expected him to. The youth came wandering down from the village, his face set. Behind him a group of young men regarded Thomas mutinously. The big man ignored them and stood up. He looked down at Benny, schooling all pity and compassion from his mind.

'Whichfella canoe bilong you?' he demanded.

Silently the boy indicated one of the dug-outs on the sand. Thomas walked over to it and slid the craft down to the sea. 'We go long Kukala this time,' he said.

⋆ ⋆ ⋆

They reached Bannion's stronghold soon after dusk. They had paddled steadily through the afternoon and early evening to reach their destination, Thomas sitting in the rear of the canoe, not taking his gaze from the youth. They did not speak.

Four men were waiting at the jetty. One of them tied the canoe to a post while the other three took Benny off into the darkness. He went without looking back. For a minute Thomas sat thinking in the canoe. Then he heaved himself out and walked to Bannion's hut. The Australian was sitting in front of his radio receiver. As Thomas came in he removed his headphones and turned round to face his assistant.

'What do you know,' said Bannion. 'I've just had a coded message from Jessop. He wants me to arrange for a seaplane to pick up an American pilot he's bringing over tomorrow. It looks as if we're going to get a look at Manno.

7

The canoe rested gently on the water in the lee of the island, one of the dozen scattered over the early-morning sea. McKinley placed his oar in the bottom of the canoe and turned to watch Senda playing out the cord of her kite.

'I've never seen fishing like this before,' he marvelled.

'We often do it this way in the Solomons,' she smiled. 'It works, doesn't it?'

The American glanced at the pile of fish at his feet and agreed. They had been out at sea for less than two hours and in that time had caught over a dozen kingfish and bonito. The kite, a contraption of bamboo and leaves, was secured to the canoe by its cord. A line and hook suspended from the bamboo fell to the water fifty feet from the canoe.

McKinley leaned back contentedly. His pilot's uniform was buried safely ashore and he was clad only in a faded lap lap. He was taller and bulkier than the average Melanesian but his skin was much the same shade of colour; even Jessop had been forced to admit that there was little danger of his being picked out by any passing Japanese.

'It's time we went ashore,' announced Senda.

'Already?' groaned McKinley. 'What for?'

'Church, and then I have to open the school for today's lessons.'

'Forget it,' coaxed the negro. 'You take the school too seriously anyway.'

'Education *is* serious, Mac, especially in the Solomons.'

'Sure, but — ' McKinley gestured at the placid blue sea and the green palms dipping in the breeze on the tiny island a hundred yards away. 'Nothing seems serious here, know what I mean? Everything's too pretty and peaceful.'

'I know.' Senda's voice was troubled. 'That's what's wrong, Mac. It's all too easy for us. We've got the sun and enough land to grow our food on and a sea full of fish, and we think it's enough.'

'Maybe it is.'

'No.' Senda's tone was definite. 'We mustn't let it be enough.' She looked almost apologetically at McKinley. 'I don't know how to say these things,' she said fiercely, 'but there is more to life than fishing and lying in the sun. The things they told me at the mission . . . '

Her voice trailed off. They were both silent as the canoe jostled lazily with the current. Then Senda began to haul in the kite while McKinley picked up his oar. Instead of thrusting it into the water he sat staring ahead.

'I never thought you people were like this,' he said frankly. 'Tell you the truth, I reckoned you for a bunch of savages swinging from the trees.'

'Most of us are by your standards,' said the girl. 'We haven't had the chance to be anything else. Just a few of us have been educated by the missions or sent to school in Fiji by the Government. Those of us who have been educated must help the others.'

'Yeah,' said McKinley non-committally.

He began to paddle for the shore with deliberate strokes.

'Don't you agree?'

'Well, I don't know,' said the negro evasively. 'I don't go much for this social conscience item.'

'What do you mean?'

'I mean that all my life I've been a black man living in a white man's country. Nobody's ever done anything for me. Everything I've done I've accomplished by being twice as good as the white men competing with me. I got no hand-outs.'

'But they made you a pilot — '

'They didn't have any choice. I was the best damn recruit they had. Anyway, they needed me. They needed all the niggers to help them fight their white man's war.'

'I'm sorry,' said the girl hesitantly. 'I don't know about these things.'

'No, *I'm* sorry. Why should you know about them? I was just shooting my mouth off. Forget it, Senda. Say, how am I doing with this paddle?'

'Very well.' The girl's unhappy expression was lightened by a flashing smile.

'We'll make a warrior out of you yet.'

'That I can do without,' McKinley assured her, but he was grinning as he spoke. 'All I want is to pick me out a good coconut tree to lie under for the rest of my days.'

Guiding the dug-out clumsily but with considerable strength he breasted a wave and ran the craft up the beach. Senda jumped out and helped him drag the canoe above the water line. She piled the fish into a woven basket.

'I'll be cooking some of these after school this morning,' she said. 'Will you come and eat with me?'

'I'd surely like that,' said McKinley. He glanced at his wrist and then realised that his watch was buried with his clothes. 'I'll keep an eye on the sun,' he promised.

He stared after Senda as she walked away along the beach, carrying the basket on her head, her full but shapely figure swaying gracefully as she moved. That was one hell of a girl, thought McKinley. He had never met one like her.

He strolled up the sand to the huts,

whistling. His skin was growing accustomed to the sun and the soles of his feet hardening with constant contact with the ground. He felt oddly liberated and at peace with the world.

'McKinley,' he told himself, 'you've never had it so good.'

Somewhere in the village a drum was being beaten to signal the imminence of the morning church service. The lives of the people were regulated by the drum. It was used to signal work-periods in the gardens, the opening and closing of the school, the approach of strange canoes and a dozen other occasions. Senda had told McKinley that such signals were used all over the islands. She had spoken of the talking drums of Savo and the fighting drums of Vanikoro. 'Our customs are very important to us,' the girl had said seriously. 'In some islands traditions are all that the people have.'

The men and women of the village were walking towards the wooden church. Those who passed McKinley greeted him pleasantly but with a certain shy reserve. The negro knew that he was an enigma to them. He had been landed on the island two days ago by the war canoe from Renbanga and this in itself had been enough to puzzle the villagers. At Jessop's instructions Renbanga men had not come ashore and as far as McKinley knew the story of Manno had not percolated to the island.

'McKinley!' Jessop came out of his hut. In spite of the early hour the young Englishman was spruce and alert. 'It's all arranged. A canoe will take you to Kukala. You can wait there until a seaplane comes to fly you to Tulagi.'

McKinley greeted the news without enthusiasm. He had been in the village only two days but he had grown attached to it and the way of life of its inhabitants. And there was Senda.

'I'll see you before you go,' Jessop was saying. 'Lucky man, you'll be back with your squadron in a day or two. I'll have one or two messages for you to — ' He stopped, staring over the American's shoulder.

'What is it?' asked McKinley.

Wordlessly Jessop pointed out to sea.

One of the fishing canoes was being paddled furiously towards the shore, its occupants shouting unintelligibly. The dugout had been seen from the church and the villagers were streaming down to the beach.

'Something's up,' said Jessop. 'Let's find out what.'

By the time the two men had reached the water's edge the canoe had reached the shallows and one of its two occupants was tumbling out and splashing ahore.

'Japani come,' he gasped. 'Twofella ship.'

An alarmed murmur went round the assembled throng. Jessop quelled it with a sharp word and rapped out a series of instructions in pidgin before turning to McKinley.

'Nothing much to worry about,' he said reassuringly. 'The Japs come over and search the village now and again. I think they pick up the signals from my transmitter. I've arranged for you to be taken to Kukala now. If you leave straight away you can be gone before the Japs come round the headland. You'll have to leave your uniform and effects here, I'm afraid. That way you'll be able to pass as a Melanesian.'

'What about you?'

'No problem. This has happened before. I'll take to the hills with my radio for a couple of days until our chums have gone.' He peered out to sea. 'I don't want to rush you too much but we haven't got a great deal of time. Welchman and Peter will get you safely to Kukala.'

McKinley saw that two men were balancing a canoe just beyond the breakers. He felt lost and bewildered. This was the time when he should make a decision but all the will seemed drained out of him. Searching through the crowd his eyes caught and held Senda. She stared back intently as if memorising his features.

'If you don't mind, old boy,' said Jessop, urgency colouring his tone. 'You might get away with it if you're caught, but if they get me I doubt I can persuade them that I'm an albino.'

The negro could see that the other man was worried. Slowly he nodded. It wouldn't be fair to risk the Englishman's life after all that the latter had done for him. Anyway, he wouldn't be gone for ever, he would see to that.

Casting a last look at Senda McKinley waded through the water and climbed into the rocking canoe. Immediately the two Melanesians began to push it through the water, gathering impetus. When the dug-out was skimming over the surface they jumped in and picked up their paddles.

McKinley looked back at the island. Jessop was already running for his hut. Senda waited motionlessly among the crowd. She did not stand out among the others but McKinley knew that he would never forget her standing on the beach with the huts and the palm trees behind her. I'll be back, the negro promised himself. I shall return. Me and Mac-Arthur both.

★　★　★

For most of the journey they were out of sight of land. Peter and Welchman were taking no chances and kept well away from the coast of Renbanga. The sun was a grossly swollen ball, filling the sky with its blazing presence and seeming to suck up all the life from the sea, leaving it an airless void. Sweat poured from McKinley's body but he continued to drive his paddle into the water, hoping that the rhythm would take over his mind and drive out the thoughts of Senda. He wondered what the Japanese would do at the village. Jessop had pretended to take it lightly but he had been worried enough. The Englishman should be all right though, he would be up in the hills by now.

As hard as McKinley worked his paddle he could not put Senda out of his mind. He thought of the tra-la-la the previous evening. Some of the younger men had caught three pigs that morning. The event had been celebrated by the whole village around an open fire on the beach. After they had eaten the meat and the accompanying yams and taro there had been music. Four of the older men had played custom tunes on bamboo pipes while the others had clapped in unison. A youth had strummed a guitar and sung the breath-takingly lovely Langa Langa love-song. Later there had been dancing — the Solomon Islands tra-la-la. Men and women had strolled in time to the music, one arm about each other. McKinley had danced with Senda. They had said little, aware of each other. The gentle moon had sprayed the white sand and in the distance breakers had crashed darkly against the reef.

A hand on McKinley's shoulder brought him out of his reverie. Peter was pointing ahead. McKinley could just make out a blur of mist-wreathed coastline. He raised a hand in acknowledgement. It looked as if the next stage of his journey was immiment.

Several hours later the canoe was nosing up an inlet overhung with creepers. It rounded a bend and floated into a small harbour. McKinley noticed a dilapidated schooner and several barges at anchor among the canoes of all sizes. Huts were scattered about the clearing on the shore. The Melanesians steered for a wooden jetty. When they reached it Welchman stood up and steadied the canoe by holding on to a post as he helped McKinley ashore.

The negro steadied himself and turned to thank the Melanesians. The canoe was already turning in mid-strcam. Welchman waved briefly and then the dug-out was weaving among the other canoes towards the harbour entrance. McKinley walked along the jetty. A crowd was forming. Some of its members were thrust aside as a stocky white man shouldered his way to the front. He regarded the pilot speculatively.

'So you're the Yank,' he commented. 'You could have fooled me.'

McKinley glanced ruefully at his lap. 'You'll have to pardon me,' he said. 'They told me it would be strictly informal.'

The white man grinned briefly and extended a hand. 'Bill Bannion.'

'Dave McKinley — Mac.'

'Pleased to meet you, Mac. Come up and have something to eat. You'll be staying here tonight. I hope they'll be sending a plane for you tomorrow or the next day. How was Jessop when you left him.?'

Bannion led the way to one of the huts, listening intently as McKinley told him of that morning's raid by the Japanese. When they entered the hut he gestured to the pilot to sit at the table before a plate of corned beef and sweet potato. Bannion watched absently as the pilot ate.

'Jessop should be safe enough in the hills,' he said thoughtfully. 'It'd take a regiment of soldiers to find him up there. As long as the Japs don't get nasty when they fail to find him, it'll be all right.'

'Are they likely to — get nasty, I mean?'

'It's hard to say. The official Japanese line is to leave the natives alone. They've come to rid the lads of the harsh hand of British colonialism, that sort of thing. On the other hand, a lot of Solomon Islanders are beginning to help the Yanks on Guadalcanal and in the West. There's the Labour Force and Vouza and the other scouts, and a few other things. The Japs don't like that.'

McKinley was about to reply when the door opened and a tall, broad-shouldered man came in. The newcomer nodded.

'You must be McKinley. I'm Sam Thomas. You've been having quite a time lately, I hear.'

'Yes, tell us about it,' invited Bannion. 'So far we've only got the story in bits and pieces.'

McKinley put down his fork and told his story from the time he had crash-landed his Seagull. When he had finished the other two exchanged glances.

'That Manno bit seemes to have caught on,' observed Bannion. 'We've been hearing a lot about it lately. They say you cured a crippled child at one of the villages.'

'I what?' McKinley racked his brain. 'There was a kid who fell down as we were getting into the canoe. I picked him up and gave him back to his mother, but he was no cripple.'

'That's how these stories start. About that Japanese patrol. You're sure it was Benny who brought it back?'

'Senda said so, and she followed him.'

'It sounds conclusive enough,' said Bannion, and Thomas nodded.

'It seems that Voli pressured the kid,' said McKinley.

'Maybe,' said Bannion. 'Now I'm going to put some pressure on him as well.'

'You mean Benny's here?'

Bannion nodded. 'We've been waiting for you to arrive to give your side of the story. We can carry on now. All right, Sam.'

'Just a minute,' said McKinley. 'What are you going to do to him?'

'That's our business.'

'Seems to me I've got a stake in this as well. If it wasn't for Benny, Jessop would never have reached me in the first place. I owe the kid that much.'

'I don't give a monkey's nut what you owe him,' blazed Bannion. 'Benny betrayed you and Jessop to the Japs. I don't care what his reasons were. If I let him get away with it somebody else might take it into his head to do a bit of collaborating. Once that started me and Sam would be dead in a month; so would every other coastwatcher. Benny's got to be taught a lesson.'

'What sort of a lesson?'

'If you must know,' said Bannion, stiff with annoyance, 'come and see for yourself.'

The three men emerged from the hut. Bannion walked to a square surrounded by huts. Thomas and McKinley followed him. Several hundred people had already gathered in silence around the perimeter of the square. Two large empty petrol drums lay on the ground. Bannion glanced quickly round the square and then said something to Thomas. The big man signalled to two of the Melanesians. They went into a hut and reappeared with Benny between them. The boy was clad in ragged shorts. He tried to square his shoulders and look defiant but his walk betrayed him. His legs would not obey the orders of his brain and the Melanesians had to half support the youth to the centre of the square. Picking up a length of rope they tied the youth face downwards on top of one of the petrol drums. He did not struggle.

McKinley looked on in horror and amazement, half-expecting the crowd to surge forward in protest. No one moved.

It was almost as if the Melanesians were accustomed to such exhibitions. The pilot's suspicions were confirmed when Bannion started to speak.

'He's using language — local dialect,' explained a voice in McKinley's ear. It was Thomas and there was an element of pride in his tone. 'Not many white men can do that, just some of the missionaries and Bannion. He's telling the people what Benny's done and why he's being punished.'

'It's barbaric!' burst out McKinley. 'What is he, a savage or something?'

Thomas's air of friendliness disappeared. 'He's got a hard job,' he said woodenly. 'He's got to keep discipline.'

Bannion finished his short oration and turned back to Benny, his hands unfastening the wide leather belt at his wrist. Wrapping it once round his hand he raised his arm above his head and brought the strap down sharply across the boy's naked back. Benny screamed once and then gritted his teeth and moaned softly as the other flailing blows cut into his skin.

McKinley flinched as he watched the sickening tableau: Bannion sweating as he smashed the belt again and again on to the sobbing boy's lacerated flesh; the Melanesians watching in fascinated silence; the dense jungle in the background. Suddenly the pilot's revulsion came to a boiling-point. He moved forward. A massive hand clasped him by the shoulder. McKinley squirmed impotently in Thomas's grip.

'You've been told once,' murmured the giant. 'It's none of your business.'

With a final bone-jarring squeeze Thomas released his grip. McKinley rubbed his aching shoulder and watched as Bannion brought the leather strap down six more times on Benny's slashed back and buttocks. Then the Australian stood back, pumping for breath, the belt dangling limply from his hand.

The men who had tied Benny to the drum unfastened the youth and lifted him gently. McKinley watched the unconscious boy being carried back to the hut as the crowd began to disperse, still in silence. The negro turned furiously on Bannion.

'You butcher,' he snarled. 'You bloody butcher.'

The Australian's expression was one solely of weariness. 'Grow up,' he said, and walked away.

8

There was a lattice of branches over his head when he looked up at the sky. Two parrots, shimmering gloriously, swooped and climbed among the trees as if imprisoned in a great natural cage. Jessop stumbled down the slope, the teleradio in its pack chafing at his shoulders. Soon he would stop and look for a place to hide it before making a final cautious approach to the village. He had been in the bush for two days, ample time for the Japanese to have concluded their search and to have left the island.

He was less than half a mile from the village. Jessop slowed his pace. Something was not quite right. Normally at this stage children would have been coming out to meet him, treating the incident as a great joke. At least he would have seen some of the women on their way to the gardens or met old men collecting betel nut. But there was nothing, just the tangled undergrowth and the trees stretching apparently to the sky. The area could have been empty or there might have been a hundred pairs of eyes keeping him under surveillance, it was impossible to tell.

Jessop kept going for a few more hundred yards and then stopped and eased the pack from his back. Looking round he selected a patch of undergrowth at the foot of a broad tree and gently pushed the radio under the thicket, scattering some more branches and leaves on top. When he was satisfied that no trace of the pack remained he started out again for the village.

The acrid smell of smoke writhing through the trees like an insubstantial herald of despair convinced him that something dreadful had happened. His heart hammering Jessop went faster, slipping from tree to tree until he came to the clearing by the sea that housed the village. For the space of an agonized minute he stood regarding the scene in front of him. Then he turned aside and vomited. When he forced himself to turn back, wiping his mouth, he could see the charred remains of the huts. As far as he could see not one remained standing. The smoke curled in the still air over the carnage. Bodies lay sprawled grotesquely among the ruins; men, women and children lying where they had been cut down by bayonets. Jessop could count thirty corpses from where he stood.

He forced himself to walk out into the deadly shambles. The blackened stumps on the left had been the school, *his* school, he thought fiercely. Dazedly he stooped over one of the forms lying among the embers. It was Senda. She was lying protectively across two children as if she had flung herself over them in a last desperate paroxysm of effort. All three were dead.

For half an hour Jessop groped his way round the site. Occasionally he stopped and fingered a piece of smoking wood or a carved bowl which had rolled free. As far as he could tell there had been little looting. The people had possessed nothing that anyone else could want.

As the initial shock wore off Jessop experienced a curious lack of sensation.

He tried to rouse himself by picturing the village as it had been before. A series of scenes passed in a montage before his eyes: canoes drifting over the waves; the young men, spear-grasping and shouting noisily, going hunting; the old men telling stories under the shade of banana leaves held by the stalk; the whole village gathered at evening feasts.

Jessop stopped, his sense of order taking over. He would have to report to Tulagi on what had happened. There would be survivors of the massacre hiding in the bush. They could tell him what had happened. Jessop wondered why the Japanese had run amok in this fashion. Had it been out of spite at not finding the radio they had monitored so laboriously, or was there a more ominous reason?

In this sombre frame of mind Jessop retraced his steps through the jungle to where he had left his teleradio. The survivors were already drifting out of their hiding-places. A crowd of Melanesians had gathered in front of the tree and more men were creeping stealthily out of the bush.

Jessop hurried forward to meet the villagers. The crowd opened out to reveal his radio. It had been dashed against the tree and shattered. The man standing over it was one of the village elders. The man's face was rigid with grief and rage.

'Whichway — ' began Jessop, but was silenced by the elder raising a quivering hand.

'No more. Youfella go bloody quick time. You takim onefella canoe, onefella man himi paddle. Go-go long white man bilong Kukala.'

The others around him growled their assent. Jessop realised that in their present state they were not far from attacking him. He had got off lightly by losing only his teleradio. Under the circumstances the elder's offer of a canoe and a guide, even though it was daylight, was generous. There would be no point in arguing. The villagers would never let him stay on the island now; nor, he discovered, did he want to stay.

'Quick time,' he agreed, turning and walking back towards the sea.

McKinley woke up with a headache and a bad taste in his mouth. He had been sleeping on a blanket in a corner of the hut allocated him the previous night by Bannion. The Australian had not spoken to him since the flogging episode, leaving it to Thomas to make the arrangments. The half-caste had brought McKinley his food but had been almost as uncommunicative. Once McKinley had tried to find Benny but had been turned back by the big man.

The American rose and walked over to a bowl of water someone had placed in the middle of the hut while he slept. As he washed his face and upper body he wondered what the day would bring. If the seaplane arrived he would be back on Guadalcanal in a couple of hours. He would be flying again in a week. His thoughts turned again to the chances of his making his way back to Senda, but reluctantly he dismissed the idea. It would be pointless going absent without leave in this part of the world. They would call it desertion in the face of the enemy. If they caught him they would throw the book at him; if they didn't put him in front of a firing squad he would spend the rest of his life in the stockade.

He stepped outside the hut. Bannion and Thomas were deep in conversation on the other side of the clearing. The former beckoned the negro who walked over to them.

'There's some breakfast waiting for you in my hut,' Bannion told him. 'I'll be obliged if you'd stay in there until the seaplane gets here from Tulagi.'

'Why?'

Bannion bridled at the peremptory question but Thomas interposed his considerable bulk between the two men.

'Over there,' he said, pointing, 'that's why.'

McKinley looked over to the edge of the clearing. Sitting under the trees, immobile in the sun, were hundreds of Melanesians; men, women and children.

'They've been coming in since last night,' Thomas went on, 'from all over the island. Some of them have walked for fifty miles. More are arriving every hour.'

'Who are they? What do they want?'

'They've heard that Manno is here. They want to see him.'

'Manno? Do they still remember that?'

'The word's spread. I talked to some of the people. There are men and women from villages which don't even believe in Manno. I've never known anything like it.'

'That's why we want you out of the way until we can get rid of you,' said Bannion roughly. 'If you start wandering about you might upset people.'

'I'd surely hate to do that.'

Bannion looked suspiciously at the negro but McKinley's face was apparently free from guile. 'Yes, well . . . Sam will take you over.'

'True now,' nodded the big man. 'I haven't had my own *kai kai* yet.'

The two men walked over to Bannion's hut. A table had been prepared with plates of pawpaw and mangoes. Thomas grunted appreciatively and sank his teeth into one of the pawpaws. McKinley swallowed a mouthful of water from a bottle on the table.

'This Bannion,' he asked. 'What's the score on him?'

'He's all right,' answered Thomas cautiously. 'He's a good fighter. That may not sound a great deal but it is to us. When the other white men ran away he stayed on.'

'Maybe he didn't have anywhere else to go.'

Thomas stopped eating for a moment as if the thought were new to him. Then he went back to the pawpaw. When he had finished the fruit he discarded it and picked up a mango.

'I don't understand Bannion,' he said, 'but then I don't understand any white man. I do know that he doesn't think much of you. He was going to ask you to help him, but now he's changed his mind.'

'What made him do that?'

'He didn't like the way you acted up when Benny was beaten. He thinks he can't depend on you to do as you're told.'

'He's right too. Do you do what he tells you to?'

'I have so far.' The big man's tone was

mild but there was an alertness about him that warned McKinley to tread softly.

'I can't make you out,' said the negro. 'This is your country but you let the white men push your around.'

'They don't push very hard. There aren't enough of them.'

'I know. If we had this set-up in the States — '

'What would you do?'

'Well, I don't know, off the cuff. But I'd damn well do something.'

'I'm sure you would.' The half-caste finished the mango and dropped the skin. 'I should try and get some sleep if I were you. The plane will be here in three or four hours. Bannion put in a top-priority call for it. He wants you well away from here.'

After Thomas had left McKinley lay down disconsolately on the camp-bed against the wall. At first he stared restlessly about him, confused images passing through his mind, but eventually he settled down and then he slept.

He was awakened by a rough hand on his shoulder. When he opened his eyes he saw Bannion's face staring down at him.

'Up,' commanded the Australian. 'The plane's due here in twenty minutes. I want you on it and away from here.'

'It'll be a pleasure,' grunted McKinley, swinging his legs to the floor and standing up. 'Don't think it hasn't been fun because it hasn't.'

'Very funny.'

'I don't hear you laughing.'

'You've got a lot to say for yourself.'

'For a nigger, you mean?'

'I didn't say that.'

'You didn't have to. I've played this game before. I've been playing it all of my life. That's what sticks in your throat, ain't it? You don't like a black man answering you back. You like 'em to fall on their faces and call you master.'

Bannion walked over to the American until he was standing in front of him. 'All right,' he said. 'All right, I *am* the master down here. Do you want me to pretend that I'm not? Without me this operation would fold up in five minutes. If it wasn't for me the Japs would be having it all their own way in this district. If it wasn't for the fact that they know I'd beat the hell out of 'em, more of the natives would be helping the Japs.'

'Man,' shouted McKinley. 'We don't care one way or the other about you or the Japs.'

'We?' demanded Bannion furiously. 'What do you mean — we? Are you trying to pretend that you're one of them?'

'I am one of them. I've lived with them. For the first time in my life I've been treated as an equal. And do you know something, Bannion, I liked it. I liked it fine.'

'Come off it,' said the Australian contemptuously. 'You may not be much, Yank, but at least you've come down out of the trees.'

'So have they. Some of them are a hell of a lot brighter than we are.'

'Who, Thomas? He's a half-and-halfer. He doesn't count.'

'No, not Thomas,' said McKinley, discarding caution in his anger. 'The teacher at the village school — Senda.'

'Senda? Now you've got to be joking. She's just another black lay. She may have squealed a bit at first but she enjoyed it as much as any of them.'

McKinley stared incredulously at Bannion. Then he stepped back and flailed his fist at the Australian. Bannion saw the punch coming but too late to slip it. He raised a shoulder and took most of the force of the blow on his upper arm, retaliating with a short jab to McKinley's ribs. The American gagged and jabbed his left twice into Bannion's face, flushing blood from his nose. Bannion swore and broke away from close quarters.

The two men circled each other warily, heaving for breath. McKinley moved confidently, his temper under control. He was taller and heavier than his opponent and had boxed with some success as a middleweight in the Golden Gloves before the war. He did not anticipate much trouble from the older man. He snaked out an exploratory lead.

A second later he was writhing in agony on the floor of the hut. Bannion had swayed inside the punch and brought up his knee with excruciating force into the negro's groin. Through mists of pain

McKinley could discern the Australian's boot swinging for his head. Somebody had just torn up the Queensbury Rules.

His reflexes had been swift enough to take him away from the full impact of Bannion's boot. The kick caught him a glancing blow in the small of the back. Squirming round he seized Bannion's other leg, toppling the Australian to the ground where both men scrabbled desperately for position. Exerting all his strength McKinley forced himself on top of Bannion, his fingers straining for the other man's throat. Bannion struggled frantically but he had exerted much of his strength in his opening burst. As McKinley smashed his elbow into the Australian's unprotected face the words of the unarmed combat instructor in recruit training, a big, glossy jock-strap, came unbidden into his mind. 'Any beef you get into, win it in the first minute, or start running.' To hell with that, thought McKinley, this is one fight I don't want to win in a hurry. Sweat it out, Bannion, I'm going to kill you and I'm going to do it by inches.

His hands were round his adversary's throat, the thumbs pressing down on the jugular. Bannion flopped helplessly beneath him. The Australian's eyes were goggling and his breathing a series of high-pitched whinneying screams. McKinley rocked forward so that all his weight was being taken on his arms. Power flowed to his wrists and hands.

There was a crash behind him as someone hurled the door open. A moment later strong hands were pulling him off Bannion. McKinley smashed back with his elbow and wriggled round to find himself staring at Thomas.

'Keep out of this!' shouted the American. 'Mind your own business, Thomas.'

'For God's sake,' muttered the half-caste disgustedly. He threw the negro to one side as if he weighed no more than a child, and hurried over to Bannion, who was rising unsteadily, his hand feeling gingerly at his throat. The Australian tried to speak once, failed, spat to clear his throat and tried again.

'Nobody asked you to interfere,' he

croaked, glaring at the big man. 'This is my fight.'

'Something's happened,' said the big man tersely, ignoring the strictures.

'What?' asked Bannion, stopping dabbing at his mouth with a handkerchief, alert at once.

There's a canoe coming up the inlet. Jessop's in it.'

'Jessop? In daylight?' Bannion thrust his handkerchief back into his pocket and headed for the door. 'Come on.'

At the door Bannion passed McKinley. He stopped and the two men stared coldly at each other. Then Bannion hurried out of the hut, followed by Thomas. McKinley hesitated and then went after them.

As he emerged from the hut a spine-tingling roar went up from the crowd at the edge of the clearing. McKinley looked over in surprise. He had forgotten the existence of the waiting Melanesians. Now there seemed to be more of them than ever. Bannion's men were doing their best to keep some sort of order but the sight of McKinley seemed to have had a galvanising effect on the waiting men and women. They were standing up, cheering and threatening to burst forward and flood into the camp. There was going to be trouble here, thought McKinley as he hurried to the jetty in pursuit of Bannion and Thomas.

He reached the wharf as they were helping the Englishman out of the canoe. His face was burnt red by the sun but otherwise he appeared unhurt.

'What's the matter?' demanded Bannion. 'What are you doing here?'

'The Japs landed,' said Jessop. 'They've demolished the village and killed thirty of the people.'

'Christ,' exclaimed the Australian. Before he could say anything else he was shouldered out of the way by an urgent McKinley.

'What about Senda?' he asked, grabbing Jessop's shirt. 'Is she all right?'

Jessop shook his head, his face pained. 'I'm sorry, Mac,' he said softly. 'She was one of the people they killed.'

McKinley gazed in stupefaction at the Englishman. Then he began to tremble.

Thomas moved forward in case the American attacked Jessop.

'All right,' said McKinley in a voice the others could hardly recognise. 'One of you raped her and the other killed her. I won't forget that.'

'Where are you going?' shouted Bannion as the American turned and began to hurry towards the screaming Melanesians.

'Never you mind,' returned McKinley over his shoulder. 'I'm going to look out for myself.'

Bannion made as if to go after the negro but Thomas restrained him. 'I shouldn't,' said the half-caste, indicating the edge of the clearing where McKinley was being greeted by the ecstatic throng. 'He's Manno, the Lord of Life. Let him go off into the bush with them if he wants to.'

Slowly Bannion nodded. 'I don't have much option.' He looked at Jessop. 'There's a plane coming in at any minute. You'd better go back to Guadalcanal on it and let the Yanks know what's going on.'

9

Jessop sat on the edge of the bed, luxuriating in the feeling of the new combat fatigues and fresh linen provided by the American quartermaster that afternoon. The seaplane had landed him off Lever's plantation on the north-west coast of Guadalcanal the previous evening. He had been interviewed by a courtly but non-committal Intelligence colonel, allocated a bed in one of the transit huts and ordered to await instructions.

He looked round the hut and wondered how long he would have to wait there. Of the six beds in the room only one of the others was occupied. He had caught a brief glimpse of a nervous-looking war correspondent the previous night, but when Jessop had woken up at noon the man had not been in evidence.

Jessop was eager to get back to Renbanga. Guadalcanal at the height of the rainy season was not an attractive spot. At the moment the base camp was swaying in the path of a monsoon. The rambling collection of huts and tents on creaking duck-boards was swamped in mud and half obscured in driving rain. Above the raging wind the sound of heavy artillery could be heard at frequent intervals. The war was being fought only a few miles away. Since the Americans had landed on Red Beach they had been inching their way inland up the ridges and along the sluggish Metanika River. The cost had been heavy. That afternoon Jessop had stood outside the field hospital and watched the wounded being unloaded from trucks like slabs of raw meat coming from a wholesaler.

He looked up as the door opened and a man bent double against the force of the wind bundled into the room out of the storm. Slamming the door behind him he straightened up.

'Inclement weather,' he remarked placidly.

'Douglas!' cried Jessop joyfully. 'What the hell are you doing here?'

'Hullo, old boy. They told me you were somewhere around. How are you?'

Jessop bounded over to meet the other man, shaking his outstretched hand. Douglas Wallace had been a District Commissioner before the war. He had not been an orthodox official but in his way he had been an effective one; shrewd and energetic with an insight into character which had served him well at times. His refusal to accept direction from the Secretariat had hindered his career but given him an enviable amount of security. It was a situation he accepted with equanimity. Wallace was a brisk, wiry man, below average height and looking less than his fifty years. Jessop had never seen him less than meticulous in his dress; even now when he removed his waterproof cape it was to reveal that the District Commissioner was clad in jungle-green trousers and tunic with a towelling cravat tucked neatly inside an American officer's shirt.

'Where have you sprung from?' marvelled Jessop, picking up Wallace's pack and carrying it over to the bed next to his own. 'The last I heard you were on Bellona.'

'I wasn't there very long. Actually I've been moving around like a raddled old whore looking for a new beat. Ontong Java, Kukunda, Nila and all points east.' Wallace sprawled on the bed and yawned. 'I came in from Lambi Bay this afternoon. There seem to be bloody Japs everywhere. I'm afraid the tone of the place has really gone down.'

Jessop shook his head in silent admiration. There was no point in pressing the other man. He would disclose just as much as he wanted to and no more.

'What about the others?' he asked.

'All hail and hearty as far as I can gather. Dick Horton's at Munda, Kennedy's fighting a one-man war around Choiseul, Martin Clemens seems to have most of Guadalcanal sewn up. The others are still keeping one step ahead of the Japs. I hear you've been having one or two patches of excitement yourself.'

'A few.' Jessop did not ask Wallace where he had obtained his information.

The latter had always been renowned for his intelligence service. As the District Commissioner relaxed on his bed Jessop told his story. When he had finished Wallace grimaced.

'I don't like the sound of your McKinley laddie. He seems the last sort of chap we want blundering around at this particular time.'

'In what way?'

'We live in parlous times, my lord. The old order changeth, and all that. Not to put too fine a point on it the image of the British raj has been tarnished a little of late in these parts. By all accounts the evacuation from Tulagi was a bit of a dog's breakfast, and there had been one or two other incidents which were less than shining examples of order and efficiency. Some of the local lads are beginning to ask a question or two, bless their little cotton socks. Why, for example, is an American army trying to retake the Solomons and not a British one? Why did all those beefy Australian planters and most British officials have it away like blue-tailed flies when the Japs landed?

169

What has a war between the Allies and the Japs got to do with Joe Soap from Small Mala? For the answers to these and other thrilling questions read next week's eath-shattering edition of the *Melanesian Mouthpiece*.'

'You're not being fair.'

'Fair? Fair? I don't have to be fair, laddie, I'm not refereeing a bloody football match. I'm just telling you the questions they're asking in the villages. What am I supposed to answer? That we've ballsed things up in Singapore and Hong Kong and pretty nearly everywhere else as well? Much they care. No, old son, all we can do is keep our mouths shut and our bowels open and soldier on regardless.' Wallace glanced at his watch. 'But before we do that I think we ought to sample the night life of this establishment. What have you got to offer me?'

'I think there's a canteen somewhere,' said Jessop dubiously.

'Do you mind, old son? These exotic revelations are too much for my tired old blood. A canteen, eh? No, I don't think so. Something a little more sedate and intimate is called for. You don't happen to know where the senior officer's mess is, I suppose? No, you wouldn't. Never mind, I have a nose for these things. I'll sniff it out for us.'

'I bet you will. Anyone would think you were suggesting a quiet stroll down to Leoni's.'

'Not quite,' said Wallace, standing up. 'No, not quite.' A thought seemed to strike him. 'By the way, you haven't seen Father Tulloch in your travels, have you?'

'That old war-horse? No, I haven't. Is he on Guadalcanal?'

'So I believe. The Bishop likes to keep pretty close tabs on him. I think he's afraid Father Dan might grab a rifle and go off into the bush.'

'He might just do that too.'

'Wallace grunted unintelligibly and shrugged back into his sodden cape, fastening it at the throat. As always his movements were neat and precise.

'I'd rather like to find the fighting Father, if you don't mind,' he murmured. 'Shall we see if we can persuade him to join us in a libation?'

In spite of the lightness of the other man's tone Jessop sensed that Wallace was in earnest. Without demur he put on his poncho and went to the door with the District Commissioner. Outside the rain rushed enthusiastically through the darkness to meet them in a solid sheet. Huddled against the wind the two men tramped along the squelching duckboards between the huts and tents. Wallace led the way unhurriedly but with a sense of purpose, twisting and turning unerringly between the rows. Eventually he reached a tent a little apart from the others on the side of the hill.

'This is it,' he said, stopping. He brushed aside the entrance flap and went in with Jessop just behind him.

The tent was a large one with rows of canvas-backed chairs on either side of a central aisle. At the far end of the tent was a dais bearing a table covered in a white cloth. In the middle of the table was a large wooden crucifix. Two men were talking quietly in the aisle of the church. One, wearing a cassock, was tall and well-built with thick hair brushed back dramatically over his ears. His companion was clad in nondescript grey flannel trousers and an incongruous floral shirt. He was slim and unremarkable in appearance, a man of about forty with aquiline features and pale eyes. It was to him that Wallace addressed himself.

"Evening, Father Tulloch. Are we disturbing you?'

'Good-evening, Douglas. Hullo, Chris. No, far from it. I was just having a chat with Father O'Flynn here. Father, I'd like you to meet Douglas Wallace and Chris Jessop. Boys, this is Father O'Flynn of the United States Army Chaplain's Department.'

The three men exchanged greetings, raising their voices to be heard above the drumming of the rain on the canvas roof and sides of the tent. While Wallace engaged the two clerics in practised amiable conversation Jessop studied Father Tulloch unobtrusively. The New Zealander had lived in the Solomons for almost twenty years. Most of that time had been spent in remote bush stations, a great deal of it in the pagan Coyu country of Malaita. Beneath his diffident, almost sedentary exterior he was as hard as forged steel and a passionate upholder of the rights and customs of the people of the islands he served. Jessop did not know the priest well but his reputation was that of a man who feared no one except his God.

'We were thinking of going for a drink?' Wallace was saying. 'Would you gentlemen care to join us?'

'I'd like that,' said Father Tulloch with some alacrity. He looked at the other priest. 'How about you, Father?'

'I'm afraid I'll have to take a rain-check,' said the big American regretfully. 'You boys carry on though. Have one for me. And thank you for your help, Father Tulloch. It's been much appreciated.'

'My pleasure,' replied the New Zealander. He looked round vaguely and then picked up an ancient raincoat lying across one of the chairs. He murmured his thanks as Jessop helped him into it.

'All set?' asked Wallace. 'Let's go.'

This time their journey was shorter.

Wallace plunged ahead like an eager pointer who had spotted a plummeting bird. After three or four minutes he was pulling up outside a Nissen hut.

'This is it,' he observed with satisfaction. 'Officer's Club. Noticed it this afternoon. You never know when these pieces of information are going to come in handy. Shall we go in?'

The three of them entered the hut. The door opened on to a partitioned recess containing rows of coat-pegs, many of them bearing dripping capes and military raincoats. Wallace and his companions added theirs to the collection before going through to the inner room.

The main club room was large and rectangular in shape. A bar tended by busy white-coated attendants ran along the length of one side. Small tables were dotted about, each with its complement of drinking, shouting officers of all ranks. Cigarette smoke rose in a cloud to the ceiling. The noise of dozens of shouted conversations blended to form an ear-splitting cacophony. Wallace stood regarding the noisy scene with considerable pleasure.

'Charming,' he declared, beaming. His eyes roved the room. 'There's a table over there. Come on, you two, that's it. Father, you sit here. Jessop my lad, you take that chair. Good. Now just wait here while I see what I can get from the bar.'

Father Tulloch and Jessop watched the short District Commissioner threading his way confidently past the tables towards the bar. Few people had noticed their arrival and through the haze of smoke and alcohol none seemed inclined to dispute their presence.

'Curious people, these Americans,' remarked Father Tulloch gently. 'At first you think they're all just children — very nice, well-mannered children — quite untouched by life. But when you get to know them you realise that it's just a gloss on them. They're insulated against life to a certain degree but it soon wears off. It wore off in the first five minutes on Red Beach for a lot of them. They did well there. As soon as they realised that there weren't going to be any icecream-making machines and Coca Cola dispensers they got down to the job. In their way they're just as much fighting men as the Malaitans; they tend to give their enemies the benefit of the doubt at first, that's the only difference. They can't help looking well-fed and healthy. Take Father O'Flynn, for instance. He looks like a Hollywood actor, doesn't he? But he's no less a man or a priest for that. He sleeps in that church tent of his in case anybody wants to see him. The doughboys go in at all hours and he's always there. Ah, here's Douglas.'

'That didn't take long,' said Jessop as Wallace bustled back to them.

'Years of practice,' confided the District Commissioner. 'Some men are at home in a library, others in a classroom. Me, I've two natural habitats — a crowded bar and a mangrove swamp.' He put a bottle of Scotch and three empty glasses on the table. 'Service with a smile, our motto.'

'Where did you get the money to pay for that?' gasped Jessop. 'I haven't been paid for months.'

'Neither have I,' said Wallace smugly, filling the three glasses with care. 'There's a fairly steady market for war souvenirs in base camps like these. I got a hundred dollars for a samurai sword and I believe the going rate is even higher for a Japanese battle flag. In fact I'm seriously considering retiring from war effort and opening a little souvenir factory. It could be a significant contribution to the post-war reconstruction of the islands.'

'Indeed,' commented Father Tulloch placidly, lifting his glass. 'Your health, Douglas.'

'Cheers, gentlemen.'

The three of them drank appreciatively. Even Jessop found himself enjoying the warming tang of the spirit. The first step on the purple path, he thought.

'Where are you going next, Father?' asked Wallace, wiping his mouth politely with the back of his hand.

'To the weather coast probably,' replied the priest softly. 'There has been a certain amount of disorder — missions being closed down, and so on. The Bishop has asked me to walk over and see what I can do.'

'Which way will you go?'

'Across the island, I think. Over Mount Austin and down to Tangarare seems the most logical way.'

The three men were silent. The route proposed by the priest involved crossing the heavily wooded central highlands of Guadalcanal in the rainy season through the battle lines and into Japanese-held territory. The odds against surviving such a trip were considerable. Father Tulloch seemed to sense their thoughts because he looked slightly embarrassed.

'It's the least I can do,' he said, brushing back a lock of hair which had flopped boyishly over one eye. 'They're good devout people over there. They'll be looking for help. I must find out how many of our fathers and catechists have survived.'

Wallace was about to reply when the door of the club burst open and a crowd of officers came into the room surrounding a pale-skinned, enormously fat man wearing an olive drab shirt and dark green trousers. He towered above the others, giving the impression of an gigantic liner being towed into harbour by a covey of anxious tugs.

'Who on earth is that?' asked Wallace, watching the curious assembly approach the bar in a phalanx while the officers at the tables, slowly becoming aware of the visitor, began to rise in excitement.

'It's that comedian fellow,' Father Tulloch informed him. 'The one who's in all those films with Carmen Miranda.' The others looked at him in surprise. 'The Americans have the films flown in,' he explained sheepishly. 'I manage to see some of them.'

'What's he doing here?'

'Giving the troops a show. He's been in the canteen this evening. I believe he's very funny.'

Jessop looked across, dimly aware of having seen the fat comedian before. He certainly seemed to be popular with the Americans. They were crowding around him eagerly, laughing delightedly at his remarks. The officers at the back were complaining loudly that they could not see the comedian. Some of them started a chant of 'Up! Up!' The dirge changed to a ragged cheer when the fat man was hoisted into a sitting position on the bar.

'Hi there,' he rasped in a corncrake voice developed against a thousand audiences in as many theatres. 'I'm glad to be here tonight. Who am I kidding? After the flight in I'm glad to be anywhere tonight.' He waited for the laugh and then breasted it expertly before it had died away. 'I almost didn't come. It's against my religion — I'm a devout coward. Say, did you hear the one about the major and the buck private . . . ?'

Effortlessly the comedian controlled his audience, the witticisms rolling from his lips but his eyes blank and without expression. Watching the scene Jessop suddenly felt uncomfortable. It was probably good of the comedian to have come to entertain the troops but he was out of place here. Some of the lean young lieutenants and captains laughing at his jokes would be going up to the line soon. Their chances of coming back in one piece were small. It was not a laughing matter.

'I laugh that I may not weep,' said Wallace quietly. He looked at his companions. 'I think we've had enough, don't you? It's time we were seeing General Kovacs anyway.'

'Seeing who?' asked Jessop.

'Haven't you told Chris?' Father Tulloch asked the District Commissioner.

Wallace shook his head. 'There didn't seem any point. It might have spoiled his evening.'

'Do you mind letting me in on the secret?' Jessop asked patiently.

'There's nothing to it,' Wallace assured him breezily. 'One of the Yankee big-wigs wants to see the three of us at nine o'clock to discuss the Renbanga position.'

'The three of us?'

'I'm afraid so,' answered Father Tulloch mildly. 'I received a message to that effect this afternoon. What time is it now, Douglas?'

'Almost nine. Time we were moving.'

The three men stood and walked to the door, unnoticed by the Americans crowding round the comedian and laughing at his jokes. Wallace and Jessop picked up their capes while Father Tulloch pursued his customary search for his coat. Then they went out into the night. The rain was still falling heavily but the wind had eased a little. As Jessop followed the other two along the rocking duck-boards he wondered what was in store for him. The mention of Renbanga had brought rushing back all the memories he had been trying to force out of his head. The picture of the razed village shuddered before him with its smouldering buildings and dead bodies.

'Chris,' said Father Tulloch's voice as if coming from a distance. 'We're here.'

Jessop looked up with a start and realised that they were standing outside one of the tents. Two American sentries in streaming oilskins were on guard at the door. Wallace spoke in an undertone to one of them who nodded and went into the tent, leaving his companion staring stoically into space. After a minute or so the first sentry reappeared.

'You're to go in,' he said laconically, jerking his head at the tent.

The interior of the tent was furnished as an office. A large scale map of the Solomons was stretched over a wooden frame. There were filing-cabinets and a number of desks. At the largest of the desks sat a tired-looking officer with a bald head and a straggling moustache. Rimless spectacles were clipped to his nose and he was looking at some documents being presented to him by a tall man wearing a captain's bars on his uniform. The older officer looked up as the three men came into the tent.

'Come in, come in,' he said. 'Sit down. Terry, take their coats, will you?' He looked at Jessop. 'You're the one I don't know, so I guess you're the Renbanga coastwatcher. Congratulations, you've been doing a good job.'

'General Kovacs — Lieutenant Jessop,' said Wallace, performing the introduction as they sat down. The general nodded.

'I've been reading your report. Very useful. A pity they flushed you out of your island. You had that airstrip really sewn up.'

'I'm sorry, sir,' said Jessop stiffly.

General Kovacs looked penetratingly at the young man over the top of his spectacles. 'Relax, son,' he said kindly. No one's blaming you for anything. You wouldn't be here if they did. OK?'

'Yes, sir.'

'Good.' Kovacs glanced at Wallace. 'How much have you told Lieutenant Jessop?'

'Nothing, sir. If you remember, I don't know all that much to tell.'

'And you're sore at being kept in the dark by an obstructive Yank. No, don't get hot under the collar. It's all right. I apologise for the cloak-and-dagger stuff but I wanted all three of you here together, Father, no doubt you'll have a fair idea of what this is about already?'

The priest pursed his lips and took out a battered pipe. He raised it enquiringly and at a nod from the general began to fill it from a pouch.

'I think so,' he said. 'When you mentioned Renbanga. It will be Sister Mary, of course?'

Kovacs nodded. 'That's right. I'd better start from the beginning though.' He stood up and stumped over to the map. 'Something big is happening on Renbanga, we're sure of that. That's why the

Japanese used such drastic measures to make sure you were thrown off your island, Jessop. From what we can pick up they're conducting a sweep right through the district to make sure that there aren't any white people left. Now why do you think they're doing that?'

'They're going to build something or launch an attack,' said Wallace.

'Or both. We think both. So that leads us to the next question. What can the Japs do from that distance. There's no natural harbour big enough for a battle fleet and it would take a year to construct one. That leaves one main alternative.'

'An airstrip,' said Jessop involuntarily.

For a moment the American's eyes rested on him. 'Correct, Mr Jessop,' he said. 'Our guess it a very big airstrip capable of sending waves of airplanes over Guadalcanal. Where would you say they could construct such a strip?'

'On the site of the old one,' answered Jessop quickly. 'It could be done if the Japanese had the tools and the labour. They'd have to cut down a lot of trees and lay the right sort of foundations, but it's a natural place for an aerodrome — a big one.'

'That's what we reckoned. It accounts for them swatting you out of the way. It also accounts for the drives they're conducting through the bush of Renbanga to make sure we don't have any more coastwatchers down there. Which we do. And not only coastwatchers. We're not worried about Bannion. From what we know of him he's big enough and ugly enough to look after himself.'

'McKinley's down there too,' said Jessop.

'We know it. A renegade nigra in the middle of a war, that's all we need. But it's not only McKinley. There's somebody else down there as well. Right, Father Tulloch?'

'I'm afraid so,' said the priest unhappily. He looked at Jessop. 'You remember Sister Mary Maria?'

'The Dutch sister from the mission at Kopni? Yes, I know her. But you evacuated all the mission stations on Renbanga.'

'We tried to. We couldn't get to Kopni

in time. The Japanese occupied it as a barracks. Sister Mary Maria got out in time with six native sisters. She's somewhere in the bush of Renbanga.'

'My God,' said Jessop in hushed tones.

'So we have a number of problems on Renbanga,' said General Kovacs, ticking them off on his fingers. 'We have to find out what's happening at the airstrip. We have to get to McKinley and put him out of action. We have to rescue Sister Mary Maria and get her out. Right?'

'Right,' agreed Jessop dazedly. 'But how — ?'

'We've been discussing that,' interrupted the general. 'We want you to go back to Renbanga and link up with Bannion again. Between you we want a full report on what the Japanese are doing down there. At the same time anything you can do to obstruct their operation, do it. Understood?'

'Yes, sir,' said Jessop, his head buzzing.

'We're sending Major Wallace with you. Not because you wouldn't do a good job on your own but because you'll need all the help you can get. I'd like to send a company of Marines down there, but I can't spare 'em. In the same way we haven't got enough airplanes to send down there on a raid. At the moment we're hanging on here by the skin of our teeth. I think that's everything. Terry here will brief you properly in a minute. Any questions?'

'I was thinking — ' began Father Tulloch, only to be forestalled by the general.

'I know what you're thinking, and the answer's no. It would be more than my job's worth if I let you go down to Renbanga. I want you to brief Wallace and Jessop about Sister Mary — where she might be hiding if she's alive, that sort of thing.'

'I imagine the odds against her still being alive are remote,' said the priest. 'We can only hope and put our trust in God.'

'Anything else?' asked General Kovacs.

'What about McKinley?' asked Wallace.

'I'd like to send a squad down to prise him out just for the satisfaction of seeing him facing a firing squad,' answered the general. 'However, that's a luxury I can't afford. If he's just skulking in the bush, leave him alone. If he's in a position to help, use him. If he's obstructive, kill him.'

'When do we leave?'

'Tomorrow. A P.T. boat will take you over to Tulagi. A submarine's waiting to take you to Kukala. The Japs haven't found Bannion's base yet. He's been warned to expect you. Yes, Jessop?'

'It will take a lot of men to construct a full-scale airport. Where will the Japanese get them from, sir?'

'We've had a message from a coast-watcher in New Ireland. Three ships and an escort of fighters left for Renbanga yesterday. We haven't got a hope in hell of heading them off.'

'What are the ships carrying?' asked Father Tulloch, puffing at his pipe.

'Building materials,' answered the general grimly. 'That and a hundred British and Australian prisoners-of-war.'

10

The journey across to Tulagi in the cool early morning was an uneventful one. Soon after leaving Guadalcanal they were passing the volcanic island of Savo. With the powerful P.T. boat thrusting through the waves at a comfortable thirty knots it was not long before the island of Ngela was rising above the horizon. Minutes later the harbour and scattered buildings of Tulagi were in sight. Throughout the journey members of the crew stood at the rails with field glasses in their hands. Only a few months ago a Japanese force had sailed unobserved through the Slot to sink three American vessels at Ironbottom Sound.

Jessop crouched behind the windshield which protected the wheelhouse, checking his equipment for the second time. He and Wallace had each been provided with an American Carbine semi-automatic rifle which carried fifteen rounds in the magazine, and a Colt 45 revolver. In the pack lying at their feet were field glasses, compasses, a change of clothing and several pairs of socks. Both men had first-aid kits. Below decks, carefully wrapped in oil cloth, was a portable ATR4A wireless receiver and transmitter, weighing less than forty pounds. It was similar to the one destroyed by the villagers. At the village Jessop had possessed both an ATR4A and a bulkier teleradio. The latter needed far too many porters to make it a viable proposition on a mobile mission like the one upon which they were embarking.

The boat slackened speed to enter harbour. Jessop stood up and walked to the rail. Before the war Tulagi had been the administrative centre of the Protectorate; now it was a small but efficient dockyard, housing a fleet of P.T. boats and acting as the base for a number of American submarines. Labourers were shifting equipment on the wharf. Among the dark-skinned Melanesians and lighter Polynesians were a number of Chinese. In peacetime the Chinese had owned most of the decrepit trading vessels crawling from island to island, bartering calico and trinkets for copra. Now most of them were employed as mechanics and fitters on the American vessels putting in for repair and maintenance.

'We're going to pull alongside the submarine and go straight on board,' Wallace informed him, coming up behind Jessop. As usual the older man was impeccably dressed. In his pressed slacks and open-necked shirt with its matching cravat he looked as if he was about to embark on a day's cruising on the Norfolk Broads.

'What do you think about it all, Douglas?' asked Jessop impulsively.

'What are we fighting for, Daddy; is that what you mean?'

'Something like that, yes.'

'Well now, there's a thing,' sighed Wallace. He lit a cigarette and joined Jessop at the rail. 'Did you go to museums much at home?' he asked, apparently at random.'

'Not much.'

'You ought to when you get back after

the war. You'll probably find me in one of them, pinned to a card like a bloody great butterfly. And it may well be the best place for me. I'm that obsolete article, a colonial administrator. There aren't many of us left now, and in ten years or so we'll be as dead as the dodo. Fair enough, I daresay the need for us will have gone. Certainly it will have if Nye Bevan and his chums have their way. We've been whipping-boys for long enough, God only knows. Sneered at by the *New Statesman*, patronised by the clever young men, ignored by practically everyone else. It's the custom to mock the Empire now and call it out of date and useless. Maybe somebody will put the record right one day, but it'll be too late then. You'll see the job out in your lifetime, make no mistake about that. There'll be no more district officers in Africa, or India or anywhere else. Quite right, too, if there are enough local lads to take our place. But if there aren't, it's going to be a shambles, and a particularly bloody shambles at that. Still, there's one consolation. I won't be here to see it. I'll be long gone as our American friends say.'

'You still haven't told me why you do the job.'

'Because I like it, of course. I like it, I think it's worth doing and I think I'm good at it. I couldn't leave the place if I wanted to now. Nobody could live for fifteen years in the Solomons without having a memory or two to haunt him; a sunset off Vella Lavella, a feast at Takwa, a canoe trip in the early morning across the Roviana Lagoon, a Melanesian choir singing the Angel Song in Motu.' Wallace looked defiantly at Jessop. 'One way and another I've had a hell of a lot out of these islands. If I can put something back now, that's all right by me.'

There was a pause. 'Thank you,' said Jessop.

'What for? I haven't done anything,' said Wallace gruffly. 'You've gone troppo. It's the heat.'

Jessop smiled and said no more. The P.T. boat had slowed to a crawl and was manoeuvring alongside a submarine close to the wharf. A gum-chewing member of the crew of the boat came up to the two Englishmen.

'Skipper says you're to go ahead,' he reported. 'He'll get your gear taken over.'

'Right,' said Wallace. He glanced ruefully at the submarine bobbing above them. 'It appears that a certain amount of agility is going to be called for.'

Five minutes later they were scrambling up the ladder leading to the deck of the submarine. A burly, broad-shouldered man in naval uniform was waiting for them.

'You must be the coastwatcher,' he said. 'Welcome aboard. My name's Kiley.'

'Commander Kiley,' acknowledged Wallace politely. 'I'm Wallace and this is Jessop. I believe we're to be your house-guests for the next few hours.'

The commander looked at his watch. 'Twelve, to be exact,' he said. 'We're ready to cast off as soon as your stuff is stowed away. Come below and I'll show you to your quarters.'

★   ★   ★

The submarine surfaced off Kukala at seven o'clock that evening. When Wallace and Jessop came up on to the deck it was still awash with water. The moon was hidden behind a cloud and the coast of Renbanga was no more than a dark and menacing shadow. Kiley stood quietly with the two coastwatchers as members of his crew scurried to get the rubber dinghy loaded and over the side.

'Are you sure you don't want a couple of my men to row you ashore?' he asked in a low tone.

'No, thanks,' answered Wallace decisively. 'If that moon comes out you're going to be a sitting duck. Jessop and I can manage.'

'If you're sure,' said Kiley dubiously. 'It's a rough sea out there. Still, you know what you're doing, I suppose. I'll tell you one thing, I wouldn't have your job for a fortune.' He extended a hand to each of the men in turn. 'Good luck.'

'Thank you, Commander Kiley,' said Wallace. 'Much obliged to you.'

A whispered word from one of the sailors brought the two Englishmen to the

ladder. The dinghy was pitching dangerously, attached to the submarine by
several ropes held by sailors crouched on
the slippery deck. Rapidly Wallace and
Jessop went over the side, clambering
down the ladder and jumping into the
dinghy. Picking up the muffled paddles
they took their places on either side of the
dinghy. Wallace whistled once. The sailors
cast off the ropes and the coastwatchers
began to row in the direction of the shore.

Almost at once water began to swamp
the dinghy. There was a heavy swell and
the tiny craft slithered helplessly down
into the deep troughs before climbing
laboriously out of them and teetering
dizzily at the apex before commencing the
precipitous drop once more. Soon both
men were soaking wet and paddling
furiously to keep the dinghy upright.
Jessop felt the fibres of his arms tearing as
he plunged his paddle into the boiling
water. Behind him he could hear Wallace
grunting with effort.

When the canoes appeared they came
like shadows. The first Jessop knew of
their existence was when a hand clutched

the side of the dinghy. A moment later a Melanesian was scrambling over the side, taking his paddle from him. Another dripping islander was doing the same thing for Wallace. The canoes from which the two men had come were balancing on either side of the dinghy, controlled by several Melanesians in each. The dug-outs shepherded the dinghy as, under the practised hands of the two islanders, it approached the coast. A final wave caught the craft and hurled it into the relative calm of the inlet. When it reached the wharf Bannion was waiting for them, accompanied by several Renbanga men carrying lanterns.

'Hi. Get your feet wet?' he asked as the two Englishmen climbed up on to the wharf.

'It was a trifle damp,' agreed Wallace. "Evening, Bannion. Some time since we last met.'

'Tulagi Magistrate's Court, 1939,' said the Australian. 'You fined me a hundred quid for shipping copra.'

'Copra that belonged to Lever's if I remember.'

Bannion grinned briefly. 'Jimmy here will take you to your hut,' he said. 'The boys'll carry your stuff over. Come over to my hut when you've changed.'

Fifteen minutes later Wallace and Jessop entered Bannion's hut. They had changed into dry clothes and checked the radio set and their weapons after unwrapping them.

'Sit down,' invited Bannion, indicating three chairs placed around the table. 'I'm sorry I haven't got a drink to offer — ' His eyes widened appreciatively as Wallace placed a bottle on the table.

'It's rum, I'm afraid,' said the latter. 'No whisky left.'

'Good on you, mate,' said the Australian with enthusiasm, fetching three mugs from a bench in the corner. 'Suddenly it's Christmas.'

The three men sat sipping their drinks. Finally Bannion pushed his mug away with an air of regret.

'All right,' he said. 'Let's get down to cases. Who's going to be in charge of this caper?'

'You are,' said Wallace promptly.

'You've got the rank and the local knowledge.'

Bannion looked surprised. 'We'll forget the rank,' he said. 'The local knowledge, yes. That's all right then. I thought I was going to have to fight you jokers over this.'

'We'll have enough fighting to do without having a go at each other.'

'True enough.' Bannion looked searchingly at Jessop. 'How about you? The last time you were here you were all for non-intervention.'

'The situation's changed,' answered Jessop. 'Now we've been ordered to search and destroy. You don't have to worry about me.'

Bannion nodded. 'As long as we've got things straight. I wouldn't want there to be any disputes once we're out in the bush.'

'There won't be,' said Wallace. 'This is a military expedition.'

The Australian refilled the mugs. 'I'm beginning to enjoy this,' he said unexpectedly. 'I never thought I'd see the day when I'd be taking two Pom officials on a bush walkaround.'

'Make the most of it,' Wallace advised him. 'It's going to be the bush then? I thought you might be using your sloop.'

'I'd like to but we wouldn't have a chance,' said Bannion regretfully. 'The Japs have put the heat on, day and night. We wouldn't sail fifty miles before they picked us up. No, we'll have to slog across the island to the airstrip.'

'Have the Japanese ships arrived there yet?'

'Not according to Tulagi radio. They should get there tomorrow morning. I suggest we start walking at dawn. It will mean moving in the heat of the day but it can't be helped. We should get there before dusk. If we take a radio we can let the Yanks know what's going on there and ask for instructions. How's that?'

'Sounds sensible. And the other two issues? Sister Mary and McKinley, I mean.'

'Nothing there,' Bannion confessed. 'To be straight with you, I've never known things so quiet. I can't get a thing from the lads. Whether the Japs have really scared 'em now or whether McKinley's put some sort of scare into 'em, I don't know. Anyway, I shouldn't think there's a hope in hell of Sister Mary still being around.'

'The chances are poor, I agree. All right, so we walk across to the airstrip tomorrow. How many of us will there be?'

'Just the three of us. It's not that I don't trust my lads but things are a bit off just now, one way and another. I'd rather we didn't have to depend on anyone else.'

'Won't Thomas be coming?' asked Jessop.

'Thomas?' asked the Australian vaguely. 'No, he's not here right now.'

* * *

Thomas moved slowly through the bush in the darkness towards the village. It had taken him two days to locate the site, two days of obstruction, misleading directions and then, finally, a hint. Now he trod carefully. He just had to make sure that McKinley was installed in the village. Once he had done that he could report back to Bannion and leave any decision to the Australian.

A twig cracked behind Thomas. The big man whirled round. Six Melanesians were standing behind him. They were holding bush knives. Thomas stood very still. Out of the darkness McKinley stepped forward.

'Hullo, Sam,' he said. 'We've been waiting for you.'

11

'Were you really waiting for me?' Thomas asked McKinley.

'Sure I was,' drawled the American. 'It stood to reason Bannion would send someone to look for me. You were the only guy likely to get here, so I waited for you. It was as simple as that.'

The two men were strolling through the village the following morning. Thomas had spent the night sleeping in a hut guarded by two of the men who had apprehended him the previous evening. At dawn a woman had brought him a breakfast of yams and water. An hour later McKinley had appeared with an invitation to accompany him. Thomas had gone cautiously, not knowing what to expect. To his surprise he had found the pilot in a friendly, even expansive mood, moving with a new assurance. He was wearing a lap lap and sandals.

'You're looking well,' commented the half-caste.

'I feel it. The life suits me. I've even got used to eating the *kai*.'

'You've retired then?' asked Thomas caustically.

'What do you think, buster? No, I haven't retired. In fact I've never worked so hard in my life. You'll see what I mean.'

The village appeared empty but Thomas could sense that many eyes were watching their progress. He said as much to McKinley.

'Oh, I've got a few men stashed away here and there,' replied the pilot evasively.

McKinley led the half-caste out of the village and through the trees to a clearing in the jungle. The area had obviously been specially prepared, trees had been cut down and uprooted, grass and undergrowth cut and dispersed. Twenty young men were standing waiting. They were all under twenty-five, broad-shouldered and well-built, ropes of muscle moving under their glowing skins. Their hair had been allowed to grow long until it stood in a bushy helmet on their heads. When they saw McKinley they did not move but an air of anticipation stirred among them.

'East coast Renbanga men,' said Thomas, eying them. 'Hunters.'

'Warriors,' corrected the American. 'Or so their grandfathers were, they tell me.'

'True now,' conceded Thomas. 'The fighting men used to come from the east coast. A hundred years ago they were head-hunters. Cannibals as well.'

'They're vicious,' agreed McKinley admiringly. 'I've been giving 'em a chance to show me what they can do. It's been like holding red meat in front of a hungry hound. These are the best of the lot. I started with a hundred and weeded most of 'em out.'

'Just like Gideon.'

'That's right,' said McKinley unexpectedly. 'Right now we're warming up for the hosts of the Midianites.'

'You know your bible,' said a surprised Thomas.

'I ought to, my father was a preacher. Not that I spent too much time in church.'

Thomas walked forward and inspected the young men. They met his scrutiny without embarrassment. McKinley had done well, the big man admitted to himself; these men were more than fit and agile, there was an alertness and a pride about them not normally in evidence among young Melanesians. Concealing his respect Thomas looked back at McKinley.

'All right, they're beautiful. So what?'

'See them in action,' invited the American.

At a word from the negro the men scattered and ran to the trees at the edge of the clearing. When they returned they were carrying bundles of bamboo canes tipped with bone. The weapons were no more than twelve inches in length and looked puny and innocuous. One of the Renbanga men hurried to the centre of the square and set up a target consisting of two crossed poles supporting a woven square of basket work tied to them with thongs.

The man ran back to the others who were standing in a line some thirty feet from the target. The warriors lifted their arms in unison. A moment later twenty throwing spears were quivering in the target and a further twenty were hurtling through the air towards it. Spear after spear hit the basket-work until they had all been thrown.

'Not bad,' said Thomas.

'They've hardly started yet.'

The training routine which followed, although fierce and sustained, bore about it an oddly practised air. As the young men with their sweat-glistening bodies stalked and ran and wrestled they did so with a grace and sense of form which was almost balletic in its effect. Even Thomas was impressed by the exhibition.

'You taught them this in a week?' he asked.

'That's the funny part of it,' said the pilot. 'I showed them some of it, sure, the sort of stuff I learned myself in basic training. But a hell of a lot of it was already there just below the surface. Once they got into the mood it just came pouring out. I guess it must be in their blood.'

'But what's it all for?'

McKinley put a hand on the half-caste's arm. 'Come over here,' he said, jerking his head in the direction of the trees. 'Those boys are liable to go on for another hour before they run out of gas.'

When the two men reached the trees McKinley sank to the ground, sprawling beneath the shade of a tall palm. Thomas lowered himself more sedately.

'You've been asking around about me,' said the American calmly. 'So what did you hear?'

Thomas chose his words carefully. 'I heard that you're a big man, the biggest in the district. Even the villages which don't believe in Manno think you're something special.'

'A god?'

'Or a spirit; there's a difference.'

McKinley shook his head wonderingly. 'The black man who fell from the sky,' he mused. 'You wouldn't credit it, would you. I guess I've just been lucky. Plus the fact that I've had some pretty influential sponsors — Jessop, Voli. Even Bannion didn't put the black hand on me.'

'He'd like to now but it's too late. You're too big; he's got to go along with you.'

'He must love that,' said McKinley, picking up a handful of dry earth and allowing it to dribble between his fingers. 'You've been around, Thomas, you know these people. How long have I got as Manno?'

'It's hard to say.' Thomas thought for a moment. When he spoke again his voice was defiant and angry. 'My people are simple. You have impressed them. If . . . ' he struggled for words, 'if you don't let them down they will follow you for a long time.'

'But not for ever. That's what I figured. The hell with it. Who needs for ever? The way I see it I've only got to keep on selling myself for as long as it takes.'

'For as long as what takes?'

'To kill every Japanese at the airstrip,' said McKinley.

There was an extended pause. From the clearing came the shouts of the exercising warriors. Trees stirred lazily in a slight breeze. A few birds swept through

211

the sky. Children could now be seen playing outside the huts of the village.

'So that's what it's all about,' said Thomas. He sounded almost indifferent but his face had cleared as if something which had been puzzling him had now been made plain.

'Now tell me I'm crazy.'

'Why should I? I don't think you're mad. The white men would, but I'm not a white man. The Japanese killed your woman. They started a blood-feud — a *dromaia*. Now you will kill some Japanese. After you have done that some of them will kill you. Then your son, if you have one, will take up the feud, and so on. Blood-feuds have lasted for hundreds of years in the Solomons.'

'You make it sound simple.'

'Things usually are simple in the islands.'

'Will you help me?' asked McKinley.

'No. Why should I. It's your *dromaia*, not mine.'

'The others,' the negro gestured around him, 'the others are helping me.'

'Because they think you're Manno. I

know you aren't.'

'If I gave the word I could have you killed right here.'

'You could. But you won't.'

'Why not?'

'Because you look like a black man but you think like a white man. You will kill a hundred Japanese because they have injured you, but you will not kill me for I have not injured you.'

McKinley looked incredulously at the half-caste. 'Are you calling me an Uncle Tom?'

'I don't know what that means,' said Thomas doggedly. 'All I know is you'll do what white men will do. I've lived among white men. I know them. You are just like them in your thoughts, believe me.'

'Well I'll be damned,' said McKinley softly. 'I never thought to live to the day when I'd be called a whitey.'

'I'm telling you, I don't see much difference except for your skin.'

'Now, look — '

'Why don't you go back to Kukala and join Bannion? He wants to attack the airstrip as well. You could do it together.'

'Like hell we could. I owe him something as well. When I've finished with the airstrip I'll deal with him.'

'Business bilong you,' grunted Thomas, giving up the attempt.

McKinley scrambled restlessly to his feet. He gazed down at the disconsolate half-caste. 'Come on, Sam,' he said coaxingly. 'I need you to help me. You understand these people, you can get through to them. They're your people. What are you doing with the whities?'

Thomas tried to hide his confusion. 'I've lived in the islands all my life,' he said. 'The white men are the bosses. They always have been. No native has ever disobeyed them and got away with it.'

'That's old stuff, buster. Haven't you noticed, there's a war on. The whities are too busy to bother us now. They need us too much anyway.'

'But when the war's over — '

'When the war's over these islands will belong to the Melanesians. There won't be any more colonies, Sam. The Limeys won't be able to afford 'em. It's happening all over. It'll be the same with

Uncle Sam in the Philippines and other places. You come in with me now, Thomas, and you'll end up a real hero with your people. You'll be the original Melanesian freedom fighter.'

'This is just talk,' said Thomas. He stood up and turned his back on the American. 'Talk,' he repeated.

'No it isn't. You know it isn't.'

'Then what are you going to do?'

'I've told you, I'm going to destroy that airstrip. But there are one or two other things I've got to do first. What do you think I'm putting that little lot through the works for? I'm getting them ready for a raid. There's a small Japanese detachment twenty miles from here on the east coast. They've got forty troops and a few hundred cans of oil. They used it as an emergency refuelling centre for submarines. I'm taking my guys down there on a night raid. If we're lucky we'll pick up enough guns and ammunition to give us a start. It'll be the first raid made by Melanesians in this whole cruddy war. You could be in on it, Sam.'

'I don't know. There's Bannion — '

215

'Bannion's finished,' said McKinley coldly. 'I've already put the word out. No islander on Renbanga is to help Bannion or any other white man. Those are Manno's orders, and they're going to stick.'

12

It was raining when they assembled at dawn in Bannion's hut. The rain pounded at the roof and walls in a drumming rhythmic beat. Beneath their water-proofed capes the men were wearing shirts and shorts, with sheathed hunting-knives in the leather belts at their waists. Wallace and Jessop were wearing boots and knee-length socks while Bannion was bare-legged and wearing sandals. Each man was carrying a carbine wrapped in cloth. In the packs strapped to their shoulders were blankets, spare ammunition and a few tins of corned beef. Jessop had been carrying the portable receiver/transmitter which now lay at his feet.

'We'll have to take it in turn to carry that,' said Bannion, nodding at the radio. The Australian seemed tense and worried.

'It's every ounce of thirty-five pounds,' Wallace pointed out. 'Don't you think we ought to take a couple of lads to hump it — until we get to the top of the ridge at least.'

'I don't. And even if I did I couldn't do anything about it. The bastards have all gone. Every bloody one of them.'

'Gone?' asked Jessop stupidly. 'But where?'

'How the hell should I know? Back to their villages, I suppose. All I know is that when I went round the huts half an hour ago they were all empty and most of the stuff in them had gone as well.'

'What about Thomas?' asked Wallace coolly, giving no sign of the concern which the news had occasioned him.

'He isn't here either. I sent him off on a job three days ago. He should have been back long since.'

'Well, well,' said Wallace. 'There's a turn-up for the book. Frightened off, do you reckon?'

'The boys might be. It would take a lot to frighten Sam, though. I don't know. There's no point in worrying about it. We've got a job to do.'

'But are we going to be able to do it

now, that's the point,' said Wallace. He forestalled Bannion's angry response by lifting a hand. 'All right, so your fellows have done a bunk. That's annoying but at a pinch we can probably do without them. However, suppose it's more than that. Suppose something has come up which has worried all the natives on Renbanga? If that happens we're in real trouble.'

'You're talking rubbish,' snapped Bannion.

'Am I? I've been in the islands a long time, Bannion. I know these people. They can be swayed — by a *velly* man, or a curse, or a custom. If something big enough came along it could throw a hell of a scare into them.'

'All right, all right. So something's frightened them off. They'll be back in a day or two. Are we going to hang around like spare tools until they do? Last night you said I was in charge of this caper. All right, I say it's time we got across to that airstrip. That's where I'm going anyway. Are you two jokers coming or not?'

Wallace and Jessop exchanged glances.

'We're coming,' said Wallace.

'All right then, let's get on with it.'

The three men emerged in the driving rain, Jessop carrying the radio. For a moment they stood in a group. Around them were the huts, quiet and empty. Beyond the huts were the trees of the jungle, climbing steeply to the ridge. Steam rose from the ground and drifted at waist-height across the clearing, coiling around the three coastwatchers. Bannion shifted his grip on the carbine in his hand.

'Come on,' he said, a trace of nervousness beneath the truculence in his voice. 'We've got some walking to do.'

★   ★   ★

There were paths in the jungle, narrow threads of beaten grass hardly visible among the densely packed trees and the writhing undergrowth that moved beneath their feet and clutched at their legs like an army of vicious green snakes. High above them the rain smashed against the tree tops, resisted by the closely woven foliage. Steam rose around the three men in a cloud.

Jessop shifted the radio from one shoulder to the other. Each man had carried the transmitter for an hour in turn, now it had come back to him. His shirt was sodden with sweat and his legs ached. The temperature must have been at least ninety degrees and after almost four hours they were still climbing uphill. He looked at the two men ahead of him. Both of them were showing signs of strain. Bannion's head was hanging and his free hand was thrust into the strap of his pack to ease the pressure on his shoulders. Even Wallace was leaning forward stiffly from the waist, an indication of his fatigue.

'We'll come to the first bush village soon,' said Bannion over his shoulder. 'It's not much of a place but we can pick up a guide there to take us to the top of the ridge.'

It took the three men another thirty minutes to reach the miserable collection of huts which made up the village. There were less than a dozen of them, dilapidated and neglected in contrast to the attractive buildings of the coastal villages. The coastwatchers stood in the space between the two lines of huts in a rough clearing on the side of the mountain.

'Empty,' said Wallace, moving to the door of one of the huts. His gaze swept round the village. 'All of them.'

'Maybe they're away hunting,' suggested Bannion hopefully.

'The whole village? In this weather? Not on your life.' Wallace raised his voice above the driving rain. 'You'd better face it, Bannion. We're on our own.'

★　★　★

They caught a glimpse of their first Melanesian that day four hours after they had left the bush village. He was a boy of no more than fifteen. Accompanied by two dogs he was probably looking for wild pigs. He blundered across the track some twenty yards in front of the white men. Bannion yelled at the youth and increased his pace. The boy gave one startled look at the coastwatchers and plunged back into the jungle. When the three men reached the spot where the boy had first appeared there was no sign of him.

* * *

They stopped for the night when they were still a few miles from the top of the ridge. They had been walking for seven hours and each man was exhausted. In an effort to escape from the torrential rain they moved off the track and forced their way through the undergrowth to the shelter of the towering trees. The ground was wet but not saturated. Taking off their capes in silence the men spread them on the ground.

'Roll on frigging death,' said Bannion. He looked at his watch. 'We've got another three or four hours of daylight left, but we're knackered. I reckon we should call it a day. Any objections?'

'None,' replied Wallace promptly. 'You're right, we're in no shape to do anything else today. How far are we from the airstrip?'

'Another day's walk. It'll be easier when we get to the top. Ten miles along the ridge and then a fairly easy descent on the other side.'

'Easy? Hardly that, laddie. Nothing's going to be easy under the present rather unpleasant conditions. Adding it all together — no bearers and a distant lack of co-operation from the local gentry — it's hardly conducive to a Cook's tour.'

Bannion did not reply. Sitting under one of the trees, his knees drawn up under his chin, Jessop watched both men carefully. They were treating each other with respect but the throbbing chord of antagonism between them could be sensed. A gamekeeper and poacher on the same hunting trip, thought Jessop with a deadening feeling of finality, it would never work. He stood up.

'I'll keep watch for the first shift,' he offered.

'All right, mate,' said Bannion. 'We'll do four hours each.'

Jessop nodded and put his cape back on. He walked away from the others. Soon they were out of sight. Jessop moved quietly from tree to tree, making his way with difficulty through the undergrowth. He was aware that any Melanesian who wished to do so could creep up on him at will, but the Japanese were as out of place in the bush as were the Europeans. He would hear any patrol while it was still some way away. The only chance that any Japanese would have of even getting this far into the jungle would be by having the track pointed out to them. Jessop did not think that any Solomon Islander would help them in this way. It looked as if McKinley had persuaded the local people to withdraw their support but it was unlikely that they would go so far as to help the Japanese. At least, he thought wrily, it would be too bad if they did; with the Melanesians actually turning against them the three of them would be dead in a few hours.

★ ★ ★

The night passed uneventfully and at dawn, unshaven, soaked and still tired the coastwatchers moved on. They walked stiffly, like automatons, but also like automatons they seemed to possess the ability to keep moving indefinitely. Before the sun was high in the sky they had reached the top of the ridge and had turned to face the north. Their progress through the jungle was faster than it had been up the steep incline but several times it came to a halt when they lost the track and had to split up and search for it. By noon the rain had stopped but that eased their condition little. The steam enveloped them as they plodded forward laboriously like men wading through water. They passed the radio from one to the other with increasing frequency. Once they stopped for a brief meal of corned beef and water from their bottles before continuing with their journey. At two in the afternoon they began the slippery descent on the far side of the ridge. Half-walking, half-slithering, they went down the wooded slope. After several hours Bannion was the first to see the airstrip.

'There it is,' he said.

The other two came up to his shoulder

and looked down. They were standing on a small wooded plateau halfway down the ridge above the narrow coastal area and the sea. The airstrip was just below them about half a mile away. Jessop moved forward to get a better view. There had been changes. The strip and hangars were still there but the entire area was now surrounded by barbed wire. Where there had formerly been a few technicians wandering around there were now several hundred white men in khaki shorts and shirts drawn up in ranks on the sand, guarded by armed Japanese.

'Well,' commented Bannion. 'They got here.'

13

In a way Thomas had quite enjoyed his week in the village. Admittedly the people were bush and not salt-water dwellers, but he had always been a travelling man and he had a knack for getting on with people. His sojourn was made easier by the fact that McKinley allowed him a great deal of freedom, putting no pressure on him and allowing the half-caste to go on fishing expeditions from the nearest reef, ten miles away, although the big man knew that he was always under surveillance.

Throughout the week other men were constantly drifting into the village. A good proportion of the newcomers were footloose young men, eager for novelty and anxious to see the Lord of Life for themselves. These youths spent most of their time at the clearing, avidly watching the twenty warriors at their war games.

Some of the visitors, however, were

older men from the remotest corners of Renbanga. They had been delegated by their communities to look upon the face of Manno so that they might tell their line about him upon their return. In the Melanesian fashion they came prepared to be thorough, bringing their sleeping-mats with them and showing no outward signs of interest in the American. They spent hours sitting under a palm tree chewing betel nut with Thomas and storying with a dignity that became their eminence.

Their talk was desultory and apparently formless but always moving inexorably towards their common centre of interest — McKinley. How many turtles had been seen off Ilo Point three days ago? What had happened to the Tikopian canoe blown out to sea in the recent cyclone? Were the white men and the Japanis still killing each other on Guadalcanal? What had happened to all the Chinese trading ships? Would Manno see to it that they returned? Would Manno help the three white men known to be watching the Japanese airstrip, or would he continue to order them to be avoided by all Melanesians? Would Manno order the people to drive the white men and the Japanis into the sea. What did Thomas think of Manno? Was it true that he was going to be at one with Manno?

To all questions Thomas gave evasive replies and his ambiguous answers were treated with respect. Thomas had not yet made up his mind; it was understandable, he was a half-caste, part white, part black; it would be a difficult decision for him to make. He must be left alone to make it. The elders were tactful men, they moved the conversation on to other matters.

Thomas made up his mind one morning eight days after his arrival at the village. He walked between the lines of huts to the one occupied by McKinley. Three tattoo-marked warriors were on guard outside the building but obviously had received orders to allow the half-caste in, because there was no effort made to stop him.

When Thomas entered the hut the American was sitting cross-legged on the floor of the hut, listening to an excited young islander. The pilot was looking harassed. His expression cleared when he saw Thomas.

'Sam,' he said with relief. 'Give me a hand, will you? I still haven't got the hang of this pidgin.'

Thomas nodded. 'Which way now?' he asked the young man. He listened carefully as the Melanesian answered in a torrent of words. The big man asked several questions and then dismissed the youth with a word of thanks. After the latter had gone out Thomas lowered himself to the ground opposite McKinley.

'He was telling you about the three coastwatchers,' he reported. 'Apparently you've given orders for them to be watched.'

'That's right. What did he say?'

'They've moved away from the airstrip and made camp on the ridge a couple of miles from the Japanese. It seems that they're in a bad way. They've used up all their tinned food and the old one is sick.'

'Sick?'

'Sounds like malaria. Most of the Europeans have it.'

'Well now,' said McKinley with satisfaction. 'That's what I call a real good way to start the day.' He looked anxiously at Thomas. 'Nobody's helping them?'

'No. They are tambu.'

'Great.' McKinley smiled thinly. 'If it keeps on this way there won't be anything left for me to do to those three when I've finished with the airstrip. To hell with them. It's you I'm interested in. What's the word, Sam?'

'If you still want me, I'll help you,' said the half-caste.

McKinley sighed in a long exhalation of breath as if a weight had been taken off his mind. He leaned across and shook Thomas's hand.

'That's all I've been needing,' he said with satisfaction. 'Someone they respect who speaks the language and knows their customs. You won't regret this, Sam. You'll come out of it all right.'

'I'm not doing it for myself.'

'No,' said the American slowly. 'I believe you. Not that it matters but why are you doing it?'

Thomas had been thinking of little else

for a week, but he still found it difficult to put his answer into words. 'I've been watching the people,' he said. 'I've been watching them and talking to them here and in Kukala for two weeks, ever since they first heard about Manno. They've changed. You've changed them, Manno.'

'*I* have?'

'Yes.' Thomas stared at the ground. 'I have never seen the people so . . . so alive. You have brought them alive. Also they have stopped thinking of themselves as west coast men and east coast men and bush men. Now they think of themselves as Renbanga men. They are different. You have made them different.'

'Not me, buddy, the idea of me. I'm just the product. Call me a totem pole, if you like.'

'I don't understand that. All I know is that for the first time in my life the people of Renbanga are united. I don't know if that is good or bad. But it is a new thing. Perhaps it was meant to be this way. Now that it is known that I, too, am with you you will be able to do anything. I don't know how this will end, Manno, but I know that it must start, and it is I who must start it.'

'Great. You're doing the right thing, believe me. Between us we'll show the people just what they can do.'

'No.' Thomas shook his head. 'You're not interested in the people, I know that. It doesn't matter. I shall be with you to see that you do not harm them.'

'Have it your way,' shrugged the negro indifferently. 'You ride shot-gun on me for any reason you like, so long as you come. That's all that matters to me.'

Thomas did not answer. He was aware of the dangers inherent in linking up with someone as obsessed as McKinley but he was convinced that he had been intended to assist in whatever design lay ahead. That McKinley was a fanatic he had no doubt; he had seen such single-minded devotion to a cause in men before. They were to be found scattered among the islands, Melanesian hermits and recluses, white gold-seekers, all pursuing their unattainable goals with a desperate intensity. With McKinley, though, it was different. He had power, more power, perhaps, than had ever been wielded by one man in the Solomons. How he would use it remained to be seen.

'We'll operate the raid tomorrow night,' McKinley was saying. 'We need those guns and I want to start this campaign off with a successful attack. I'd like you to come with us, Sam.'

Thomas nodded. 'I'd better start getting the things together,' he said standing up.

'Things — what things? We may be able to find you a spear, but that's about all we have.'

'I'll take the spear, and use it. But there are more important things. We have to have them before we can even leave the village. We need a pig, a fighting-stick and an eagle.'

★   ★   ★

There were at least six hundred spectators assembled on the four sides of the clearing, all of them men. No women or children were to be seen. The twenty young warriors were drawn up in two ranks of ten in the centre of the square. Each man was wearing a lap lap and clutching a dozen of the small cane throwing-spears. The bodies of the warriors were bedaubed with lime and mud. Their hair was brushed upright in the traditional bushy warrior's helmet. Through each man's nose protruded a sliver of sharpened bone.

On a stool in front of the warriors sat McKinley. He was wearing his customary lap lap. Orchids were plaited in his hair and he was being protected from the heat of the afternoon sun by two young men holding bannana leaves above his head. They moved the leaves delicately, weaving intricate patterns in the air. The only sound that could be heard was the squealing of a pig in a crude cage. Thomas and two elders stood behind the cage. In another cage, ten yards away, was a somnolent eagle. The half-caste and a squad of helpers had spent the previous day catching and preparing both creatures. Now it was time for the war song.

It was started by one of the elders in a high cracked voice. After two notes it was taken up by all the assembled men. The song rose full-throated to the trees of the jungle. Thomas barely repressed a shudder. This was the first time he had heard the Renbanga war-chant. It was an eerie experience.

At a signal from the second elder the twenty young warriors began to shuffle from side to side, their hands extended in front of them. As they swayed they began to stamp their right feet hard on the ground. The stamping increased in speed as the war-chant approached its climax. Suddenly there was a loud shout and then silence. The warriors stood still.

Four men ran forward from the side of the clearing and opened the gate of the cage containing the pig. The animal was wrapped in tough creepers which the men used to secure a purchase on its body. The pig squealed but struggled only intermittently. Running, the four men approached McKinley, holding the pig up as if for his inspection. The American rose from his stool. Thomas walked forward and handed him a hunting-knife. The men pulled back the head of the pig, exposing its throat. With a steady hand McKinley drew the edge of the blade across the beast's throat. The pig screamed desperately as the blood spurted out. The four men dropped the carcase to the ground where it writhed in agony for a moment and then was still.

With every eye upon him Thomas walked to the cage containing the eagle. His lips and throat were dry. This was the most important part. If it went wrong the warriors would still go forth on their expedition but it would be as men condemned to death. Pausing for his hand to steady he lifted the door of the cage. At first the bird did not move. Then, shuffling like a very old man, it walked out of the cage. For a few seconds it stood blinking its hooded eyes in the glare of the sunlight. The assembled men watched it intently, willing the bird to approach the carcase of the pig. At first the eagle seemed content to bask in the heat but then its head began to move jerkily. It saw the pig. In a series of ungainly hops it lurched across the ground to the carcase. Then it buried its head in the blood-soaked pig.

An exultant roar went up from all the onlookers. The fighting eagle had accepted the blood sacrifice offered by Manno. The auguries for the raid that night were favourable. Amid the din Thomas drew close to McKinley. The American seemed unperturbed but there were small beads of perspiration on his forehead.

'We're running in the money,' he murmured. 'For a minute I thought that overgrown canary of yours was going into the wild blue yonder.'

Thomas concealed a smile. The chances of the eagle failing to go to the pig had been minimal. Under the half-caste's guidance the bird had been drugged and starved and its wings had been clipped. It could not have flown away and its hunger had drawn it to the carcase of the sacrificed beast.

It was a good enough beginning, thought the half-caste. Now the result of the raid would depend on how well the warriors fought and on how successfully they were led by McKinley.

★   ★   ★

The journey down the ridge that evening took the war-party three hours. The warriors left the village as the sun went down, led by McKinley and Thomas. Before setting out each of the young men had filed past a mat and picked up his twelve small throwing spears. Immediately after the sacrifice of the pig the tips of the spears had been soaked in a pot of the killing poison prepared by the two oldest men in the village. Only they knew the secret of the preparation. The poison was never used in the hunting of animals because it entered the system and made the beasts uneatable. The killing poison was used only for the hunting of men. With the exception of one or two bush blood feuds it had not been needed within living memory.

Neither McKinley nor Thomas wore any fighting marks, McKinley because he was above such things and Thomas because as a half-caste he was not entitled to them. Thomas carried a heavy hand-spear while the American was bearing a ceremonial Renbanga fighting-stick, presented to him after the sacrifice by one of the elders. The stick was delicately carved with a weighted head, decorated with mother-of-pearl.

After the official leaving of the village one of the young men took McKinley's place at the head of the file. Three more fanned out and ran ahead to act as scouts in the unlikely eventuality of there being any Japanese night patrols in the vicinity, while two more followed a hundred yards behind the main party.

They all moved quietly and with economy. Thomas found himself surprisingly calm. He estimated their chances of success at being fifty-fifty, and no man could ask for more than that in a war. The Japanese would be well-armed and thoroughly entrenched but the attacking party would have the element of surprise in its favour. The rest would depend on the fighting capacity of the participants.

After several hours the path widened

sufficiently for a while to allow two men to walk abreast. McKinley dropped back until he was at Thomas's side.

'I've been down here a couple of times lately,' he confided in a murmur. 'I don't think it's going to be difficult. Not a pushover, but not difficult. The Japs don't really expect an attack at all this far from Guadalcanal, but if it does come they think it'll be from the sea. The last thing they anticipate is a boot up the arse like this.

'How many Japanese did you say?'

'About forty of the bastards. As I see it, when we get into their camp half the lads create havoc while the rest of us grab what guns and ammunition we can and get the hell out of it.' He cocked an eye at the half-caste. 'Something wrong with that?'

'Bannion used to plan things more exactly.'

'He had more practice,' said the negro. 'I'm new to being a god.'

An hour later they reached the Japanese camp. It was situated at the head on an inlet, bounded on one side by the sea and on the other three by a cursory barbed-wire fence. There was a gate in the fence with a small guard-house to one side. Also placed inside the wire were several wooden towers equipped with searchlights which searched the surrounding bush at sporadic intervals. There were a number of wooden huts at the water's edge. One larger and more substantial building presumably housed the fuel for visiting submarines. The undergrowth between the wire and the edge of the jungle had been levelled at one time but had been allowed to grow again. In the pale light of the moon two soldiers were patrolling outside the perimeter of the wire, rifles slung carelessly over their shoulders. McKinley suddenly nudged Thomas.

'Watch,' said the American softly. 'Watch and follow.'

The first five warriors went across the intervening ground quickly, wriggling on their stomachs like enormous serpents. Thomas tried to follow their progress but lost them after the first five seconds. Guessing what would come next he focused his gaze on the sentries.

Both Japanese went down within a few seconds of each other, neither uttering a sound. The poison on the tips of the spears must have acted at once. Thomas heard McKinley grunt with approval. Almost at once ten more warriors were crawling across the ground towards the main gate. Thomas had grown accustomed to the light now that they had left the shelter of the trees. He saw that the gate was ajar to facilitate the passing of the soldiers when they came off watch. The guards who were off duty would be in the guard-house; if only two men at a time were out it meant that the total guard strength would be less than ten. There were now fifteen warriors within striking distance of the gate. The only question remaining was whether they could get into the guard-house before anyone set off an alarm.

The seven men remaining at the edge of the trees threw themselves to the ground and buried their faces in the earth as a shaft from one of the searchlights cut a swathe across the area. It passed harmlessly over their heads and then vanished as the searchlight was turned off with a loud click.

'Right,' said McKinley. 'When they go in through that gate we run like deer across to join them.'

Thomas concentrated all his attention on the gate. Once he thought he could discern a brown body writhing through the entrance but he could not be sure. For the space of several minutes nothing seemed to happen. Then with a sharp report the door of the guard-house burst open and a flood of bodies could be seen pouring into the room. At the same time McKinley leapt to his feet and sprinted for the gate, followed closely by Thomas and the five remaining warriors.

As he pounded across the open space Thomas hunched his shoulders, expecting at any moment to hear a machine-gun opening up and to feel the bullets tearing through his body. To his surprise he found himself outside the guard-house, with the rest of the camp still shrouded in silence and darkness. McKinley issued a word of command and the five warriors took up defensive positions around the guard-house, facing outwards. Thomas followed the American into the guard-house.

The scene there was oddly peaceful. Eight Japanese soldiers lay contorted in grotesque attitudes of death on the camp-beds and the floor of the hut, but there were no outward signs of a struggle. The warriors were waiting expectantly in the aisle between the beds. They looked proudly at McKinley as he entered.

'Good work,' he said. 'No trouble, huh?'

'The searchlights,' said Thomas impulsively, remembering the towers outside. 'We've got to get rid of the guards there.'

'Relax, it's all been taken care of,' McKinley advised him. 'These boys waited until two of them had climbed the towers and killed the sentries there before they came into the guard-house. It looks like we've got it made.'

McKinley was right, thought the half-caste. With the guards slaughtered and the rest of the camp still oblivious it looked as if the most dangerous part of the raid was already over.

'I want you to speak to these guys,' McKinley told Thomas in a confiding tone. 'Tell 'em there are four huts, and each one's got ten Jap soldiers sleeping in it. I want the boys to go to each hut in turn and use those spears of theirs. The huts are open-ended, so there's no problem about getting in. Will you tell them that?'

Obediently Thomas turned to the warriors and passed on McKinley's instructions. Although outwardly they were impassive Thomas sensed that the men were exhilarated and almost dangerously excited by their success. He wondered if they were getting too worked up and voiced his fears to McKinley. The latter nodded.

'You're right,' he commented briefly. 'Tell them I don't want any donnybrook. All I want is some right sneaky killing. You pass that on to them. Hut to hut with their spears, no more. OK, tell them good luck from me.'

Thomas did so and the warriors grinned and glided out of the hut.

McKinley watched them go and then turned to Thomas.

'This is where we earn our keep,' he said. 'From what I saw there are three officers. Two of them share a hut and the boss-man has one to himself. We'll take care of the double-act first.'

Thomas followed McKinley across the parade-ground of the camp. To his right he was conscious of the shadowy forms of the warriors as they entered the first hut. The fact that the Japanese soldiers would be murdered in their beds did not worry him. If a man went to war he had the right to kill his enemy in any way he desired, that was the custom. He was slightly surprised that McKinley was condoning such methods, in Thomas's experience Americans and Australians tended to be squeamish, but it was a sign of the negro's determination that he was allowing the warriors to creep from hut to hut with their poisoned throwing-spears.

McKinley stopped outside a small hut set apart from the others. He glanced at Thomas to make sure that the half-caste was ready. Thomas raised a heavy stabbing-spear. McKinley nodded and kicked the door of the hut open and leapt into the room, with Thomas only a fraction of a second behind him. There were two men sleeping on camp-beds in the room. The one nearest the door raised a bewildered head. Thomas steadied himself and brought the spear down with all the force he would have used when stabbing a shark. The officer gurgled once and fell back. Thomas wiped his spear on the blanket covering the bed and looked across at McKinley. The American was already on his way back to the door. The Japanese he had stabbed had not even moved.

Outside on the parade-ground McKinley broke into a run, making for another hut a hundred yards away. Thomas stopped to check on the movements of his warriors. They were just emerging silently from the second of the four huts and slipping into the third. So far not a sound had been heard. Reassured, Thomas hurried after McKinley, who was already disappearing into the hut occupied by the commanding officer of the camp.

For a few seconds the American was out of sight and Thomas increased his pace. As he drew close to the hut the crack of a revolver being fired echoed across the camp. His heart thumping desperately, Thomas hurled himself into the hut, raising his spear.

McKinley was standing over the form of another Japanese. The officer was sprawled inertly across his bed, blood spreading across the front of his pyjamas. His eyes stared sightlessly at the roof.

'Are you all right?' panted the half-caste.

'Sure. This cat had quick reflexes, is all. Not quick enough though. He'll have woken the others up, that's for certain. Come on, let's go and see the damage.'

The revolver shot had awoken some of the soldiers in the fourth and last dormitory hut. As McKinley and Thomas watched from the other side of the parade ground some of the Japanese tumbled sleepily out of the barracks. They were met with a shower of spears from the warriors emerging from the third hut. The Japanese crumpled and fell. Leaping over their prostrate bodies the Melanesians charged into the huts. There was the sound of confused shouting and then silence.

'No trouble,' said McKinley. 'You could say that the situation was under control. Let's go and see for ourselves.'

By the time the two men reached the hut the warriors were coming out, grinning wolfishly. McKinley nodded approvingly before turning to Thomas.

'There might be some more sentries watching the sea,' he said. 'It's not likely, and if there were they'll probably be five miles away and still running by now. All the same we'd better make sure. Send half a dozen of them to search the beach, Sam. Then I want the rest of them to collect every weapon they can find and make a pile here. While they're doing that we'll take a stroll round.'

Thomas relayed the negro's instructions, taking care that the warriors understood in particular what hand grenades were and how they should be handled. When he had finished the Melanesians assented cheerfully.

One of them shuffled his feet in the dust and muttered something sheepishly to Thomas. The latter turned to McKinley.

'They say they understand,' he reported. 'But they want you to let them have two things. They want to be allowed to keep the Japanese bayonets.'

'Fair enough,' nodded the American. 'What's the second thing they want.'

Thomas swallowed. 'They want you to let them have the Japanese heads.'

'They what?'

'Their ancestors were head-hunters. They think it would be a good tradition to bring back.'

McKinley thought for a moment. When he spoke his voice was harsh. 'Why not?' he asked. 'If they want the heads they can have them — but after they've gathered those weapons.'

Again Thomas passed on McKinley's words. The delighted warriors at once fanned out in their search for the weapons. Thomas waited for a time to see that they knew what to do, and then walked after McKinley.

'We'll sort out the guns and take the ones we want back to the village,' said the American. 'I don't want to count our chickens, but I'd say we were home and dry. How far away is the nearest Japanese camp?'

'About forty miles,' Thomas told him.

'That's what I reckoned. So unless there's a ship off the coast or a patrol in the bush, nobody's going to disturb us. Let's take a walk down to that shed by the jetty. I want to look at the fuel they've got stored there.'

Thomas muttered a reply. The reaction to the killing was beginning to set in and his hands were trembling. McKinley, on the other hand, was showing no signs of strain. The American eyed Thomas quizzically.

'Something bothering you?'

'Doesn't it worry you?' burst out the half-caste. 'We've killed forty men tonight.'

'No, it doesn't worry me. I've seen guys killed before. Where I was raised you were ahead of the game if you got through a day without being beaten up or knifed.

My daddy was a Harlem preacher. He thought it was his duty to spend his life helping people who didn't give a damn for him or his religion. He pretty near broke himself putting me through college. And for what? Because he reckoned that if I got myself an education I wouldn't have to step off the sidewalk every time a white man came along. Man, was he ever wrong.'

'The Japanese aren't white men,' Thomas pointed out quietly.

'Makes no difference. Once you've honed a hate inside you it's there like a knife, ready to be used on anybody who comes along. Besides, the Japs killed Senda.'

'Your woman?'

'She never was my woman.' McKinley was staring straight ahead as they walked. 'She might have been if they hadn't killed her. As it was we only had a couple of days together. Would you believe me if I told you that those two days mean more to me than the other twenty-seven years of my life?'

The two men walked on in silence.

Presently they reached the jetty. McKinley looked with interest at the shed built at the water's edge. He tried the door, which did not budge.

'That'll be the fuel,' he mused. 'Sam, you've got the weight, see if you can break in.'

Thomas put his shoulder to the door. It withstood his first two charges but yielded with a splintering crack at his third attempt. As he stood massaging his bruised shoulder McKinley walked past him into the shed. Row after row of drums and containers were stacked as high as the roof.

'Go back and see how the guys are getting on. I want them to carry away as much ammunition and all the guns they can. We don't have to hurry back so make sure they're really loaded. When you've done that get them out of the camp. Send one of them to fetch back the ones we sent down to the beach. When they've all gone, come back here with a couple of grenades.' McKinley grinned crookedly. 'We'll go out with a bang.'

Thomas hurried away. Back on the

parade-ground the warriors had assembled all the weapons they had found. Thomas counted two machine-guns and over forty rifles and revolvers as well as a number of grenades and a dozen boxes of ammunition. Thomas noticed that by this time every warrior was wearing a Japanese webbing belt with a bayonet thrust through it. The half-caste sent one of the Melanesians to fetch those who were patrolling the beach and turned to organizing the carrying of the weapons and ammunition to the main gate of the camp. With a little help they should be able to get the entire consignment at least halfway up the ridge and send for help from there.

At the gate the door of the guard-house was open, swinging on its hinges. Thomas could see the dead bodies of the sentries. One of the Melanesians stopped in the act of stacking ammunition-boxes and fingered his bayonet expressively. Thomas nodded. Stooping, he picked up two grenades and walked away, leaving the islanders to the custom of their ancestors.

He found McKinley waiting outside

the fuel shed. The American was squatting on his haunches, staring along the shore of the inlet. He rose as the big man approached.

'Something's happening over there,' he indicated. 'I heard voices. I don't know what . . . ' His voice trailed off as he gazed into the darkness.

Thomas moved forward in order to get a better view. McKinley was right, people were moving about at the edge of the creek. Thomas's grip tightened on his spear. If there were any Japanese out there he and McKinley were completely exposed. The voices grew louder. Thomas relaxed. He could make out the marking on the body of one of the warriors. A moment later the man was standing in front of them. With him were two other Melanesians, middle-aged men in shorts and shirts. Thomas questioned the warrior and translated the man's answer for McKinley's benefit.

'He found these two men locked in a hut,' he said. 'They're native catechists from one of the Catholic mission stations. The Japanese caught them and locked them up.'

'All right,' nodded McKinley. 'We'll take them back to the village. Now get them the hell out of here before I let these grenades go.'

Before Thomas could speak one of the catechists pushed forward, talking urgently. After the first few words the half-caste listened with frowning concentration.

'What is this?' demanded McKinley impatiently. 'We haven't got all night.'

'This is important,' said Thomas sharply.

The surprised American fell silent until the Melanesian had finished. When Thomas had spoken reassuringly to the catechists and the warrior had bustled them both away in the direction of the gate, the American spoke again.

'What was that all about?' he asked.

'He said there are some sisters from the mission hiding in the bush,' said Thomas. 'One of them is a European.'

McKinley looked shaken but recovered quickly. 'Very interesting,' he said sardonically. 'Only right now I'm more concerned in doing a demolition job than conducting a missing person's bureau. Is that all right with you?'

'Yes, that's all right,' said Thomas quietly.

'I'm glad to hear it. Give me those grenades.'

McKinley and Thomas withdrew until they were twenty yards from the open door of the fuel store. Removing the pins McKinley lobbed both grenades with great care and precision into the shed. As the first of a dozen explosions rocked the camp and the red glare illuminated the sky the two men turned and ran for the gate.

14

It took Wallace three days to recover from the effects of his fever. For five days before that he had shivered beneath the pile of clothes heaped upon him by Jessop and Bannion. They had constructed for him a make-shift shelter of branches covered with palm fronds and placed against the broad trunk of a tree in the jungle. On the morning of the eighth day he crawled out of the shelter and stood up unsteadily. Jessop, who had been sprawled under a tree cradling his carbine, scrambled to his feet.

'You shouldn't be out here,' he said concernedly. 'You've been ill.'

'I sincerely hope I haven't been as bad as you look.'

Jessop laughed shortly and fingered his week's growth of beard. 'You look worse,' he said. 'How are you feeling?'

'All right. I've had malaria before. This wasn't a bad dose as they go. Where's our antipodean friend?'

'Bannion? He's gone walkabout to one of the villages to see if he can find bearers to carry you back to Kukala.'

'Not necessary. Anyway I thought we were *persona non grata* in this part of the world.'

'So we are.' Jessop passed a hand wearily over his face. 'We're in a pretty bad way,' he admitted. 'We've run out of tinned food and we're living off what we can grub up out of the soil and a few coconuts. We can't get close enough to the airstrip to be able to contact any of the prisoners.'

'Have you been on the radio to Tulagi?'

'Yes. They can't help us. We've been radioing in situation reports every day but the Yanks can't spare any aeroplanes for an air-strike. They've repeated their instructions for us to delay the building of the strips as long as possible.'

'Easier said than done.'

'Exactly. Bannion's decided that we ought to go back to Kukala. We may find some of the islanders around there willing to talk to us and tell us what's happening.

Something's going on, that's certain. There was a hell of an explosion five or six days ago.'

'Where from?'

'Somewhere on the east coast,' said Jessop vaguely. 'The Lord knows where.'

'You sound knackered, old son.'

'The week has been a bit fraught,' admitted Jessop.

'We had to move you out in a hurry once or twice when the Japs sent patrols up the ridge, and Bannion's been acting up in a general anti-Pom fashion.'

'I do seem to have been missing out on things. As a matter of interest, when did I first go under?'

'A week ago. We'd just got you up here when you collapsed.'

'That must have added to the gaiety of nations. I haven't contributed a great deal to the excercise so far, I must say.'

'You're not kidding! The pair of you are about as much use as two hind tits.'

The two Englishmen swung round. Bannion was stepping out from the shelter of the trees. His shorts and shirts were sweat-blackened and badly torn.

Like the other two he had not shaved for a week. His red-rimmed eyes were bitter as he moved towards them, unslinging his carbine from his shoulder.

'Whoring cowsons,' he snarled. 'The whole bloody Japanese Army could have moved in on you pooves while you were poncing about.'

'Give it a rest, Bannion,' pleaded Jessop. 'I've had just about enough of you lately.'

'You have, have you?' asked the Australian, shivering with barely contained fury. 'Well, that makes it mutual. This whole bloody issue has been the biggest fiasco I've ever been on. You Poms have been a pain in the arse from the start. One of you has been bludging sick and the other still wants his nappies changed.' He glared at Wallace. 'I hope you can walk, mate, because nobody's going to carry you back, that's for sure.'

'Couldn't you get any help?' asked Jessop.

'Of course I bloody well couldn't. I never expected to. I walked as far as Kiboni. That's the biggest village in the bush around these parts. The natives didn't even bother to run away this time. They just told me they'd had orders that the white men weren't to be helped. Cheeky buggers! I'd have put my boot into 'em for two pins.'

'But you didn't?' asked Wallace anxiously.

'Too true I didn't. I wasn't going to ask for a spear up my jackson.' Bannion cast a jaundiced look around the tiny clearing. 'We'll bury the teleradio here. We'd never get it back to Kukala in our state. Jessop, look after that, will you?'

'No, wait,' said Wallace urgently. 'Let's go and have one last look at the airstrip.'

'What the hell for?' asked the Australian disgustedly. 'There's nothing for us there.'

'Probably not, but I'd like to see it. You never know, the situation may have changed since you last saw it. It wouldn't be more than a couple of miles out of our way on the route back to Kukala.'

Bannion hesitated. 'All right,' he said ungraciously.

'I'm telling you though, you're wasting

your time. Jessop, I thought I told you to bury that radio?'

★　★　★

Four hours later the three coastwatchers were lying on their stomachs on the plateau watching the activity on the site of the airstrip below. Wallace could see that there had been a number of changes in the week since he had last been on the plateau. The strip had been enlarged and trees extending inland for fifty yards had been cut down and were being towed away by brute force by the British and Australians toiling like ants below them. Forty or fifty Japanese guards were dotted around the site, each man armed with a rifle.

'They've had to remove the barbed wire in order to cut those trees down,' Wallace pointed out.

'What about it?' grunted Bannion.

'I think one of us could get down there to one of the groups of prisoners,' said Wallace. 'We could get them to pass the word that we're here and that we're going to do our best to slow down the operation.'

'You're out of your mind,' retorted Bannion. 'In the first place we can't slow down the building. In the second we couldn't get near any of the groups.'

'I think we could,' said Wallace obstinately. 'If they knew that we were here it might encourage them to slow things down themselves.'

'Don't be so bloody stupid,' said Bannion cuttingly. 'That's about all you're good for, sitting on your backside and coming up with crazy ideas.'

'We ought to be getting back to Kukala, Douglas,' said Jessop gently. 'You've been ill — '

'I've been ill on tour before. It's never stopped me doing my job,' said Wallace stiffly.

The three men lay on their faces, regarding the scene below them. Jessop concentrated on the group nearest the edge of the jungle. There were six men in tattered shorts prising a tree stump out of the ground with crowbars. The closest guard was about ten yards away, half-asleep in the shade of a pile of timber. A really determined prisoner would have a good chance of slipping away into the bush, decided Jessop. And what good would that do? A white man on his own would die in a week.

'I'm going down to take a closer look,' said Wallace suddenly.

Before the others could stop him the Englishman had wriggled to the edge of the plateau and had begun to ease his way down the preciptous and thickly wooded incline. Bannion swore horribly and went after him. Jessop hesitated and then followed the other two.

Fifteen minutes later they reached the foot of the incline. The trees had been thinned out here and they could see the prisoners-of-war working out in the sun about fifty yards away.

'It's useless,' hissed Bannion. 'We can't contact any of them. Come on, let's get back.'

Wallace looked about him, pale-faced and irresolute. Then he was running from tree to tree towards the prisoners. He disappeared among the undergrowth and then came into view again near the clearing. Jessop glared at Bannion. It was all the Australian's fault. His needling contempt had incited the Englishman into making his ludicrous attempt. Beneath his urbane exterior Wallace had been acutely sensitive about being the oldest man on the expedition. Ashamed of having succumbed to malaria and taunted by Bannion he was seeking this way of proving himself. Jessop felt sickened by the futility of Wallace's action. The gesture was a senseless one and Wallace must be aware of it.

'The guard!' said Bannion, almost sobbing with vexation. 'He's seen something.'

The soldier who had been dozing by the pile of timber was on his feet and staring fixedly at the jungle. He moved forward uncertainly, unslinging his rifle and cradling it in his arms. He passed the group of prisoners and muttered an instruction to them. The men went on with their work, studiously not looking up. The guard increased his pace and then broke into a run, shouting as he went. Other soldiers, alerted, began to close in. Wallace halted, realising the impossibility of his position. He turned and started to run back towards Bannion and Jessop. The leading soldier stopped and raised his rifle, firing twice. Wallace staggered and reeled, cannoning into a tree and then sprawling on the ground, his limbs threshing.

'Sod this for a game of toy soldiers,' snarled Bannion, his face working in a paroxysm of rage. 'Come on, we can drag him back.'

The Australian leapt out from behind the shelter of his tree and began to zigzag towards Wallace's fallen body, firing his carbine at random. Jessop watched, unable to move. There were thirty Japanese soldiers in the jungle. Two of them fell before Bannion's fire and then a fusillade of shots ripped into the coast-watcher's body, slamming him to the ground only a few yards from Wallace. As the Japanese swarmed over the two white men Jessop turned and fled blindly into the jungle.

15

The day that Sister Mary Maria and the six Melanesian sisters entered the village it was as if they were accompanied by fife and drums. The Dutch sister led her dusty, sweat-stained band out of the bush at eleven in the morning. Thomas was waiting at the edge of the village.

'Hullo, Sam,' Sister Mary greeted him. 'It's been some time since we met.'

Thomas grinned. He liked Sister Mary even if he was in awe of her. It was typical of the woman that she should adopt such a matter-of-fact attitude after the experiences she must have been through recently. She was a small, brisk woman in her forties, wearing the heavy white robes of the Marist order. The Melanesian sisters were clad in blue habits.

'It's good to see you again, Sister Mary,' said Thomas sincerely. 'I'll take you to see Manno.'

'So it's true,' said Sister Mary reflectively. There was only a slight trace of accent in her English. She frowned. 'The guides you sent told us about the Lord of Life but I thought perhaps it was just some story they'd picked up. Sam, will the people here look after my sisters?'

'Of course. The women are waiting to give them food and shelter.'

'Good.' Sister Mary spoke rapidly in dialect to the tired-looking Melanesian nuns. She watched approvingly as the women of the village enveloped them and led them away to the huts.

'I'd like to talk to you, Sam,' she said when she was sure that all the sisters were being looked after. 'Is there somewhere we could go before I meet this Manno of yours?'

Thomas nodded, concealing his surprise, and led the Dutch sister to a lean-to shelter constructed against a tree. Sister Mary sat on the roughly hewn tree-trunk stool while Thomas squatted on the ground.

'First of all, thank you for rescuing us,' said Sister Mary. 'It was quite a surprise when your guides caught up with us in the bush.'

'How long have you been hiding?' asked Thomas.

Sister Mary shrugged. 'Three or four months. The people have been very good to us. They've been passing us on from village to village. We did have two catechists with us — Thomas and Emanuel — but the Japanese caught them. It happened near Nambi. A patrol stumbled across us and Thomas and Emanuel led the Japanese away from the rest of us. They never came back so I suppose the Japanese shot them.'

'No, they didn't shoot them. They caught them and beat them up to make them say where the white sister was, but they didn't talk.'

'You mean that Thomas and Emanuel are still alive?'

'They're waiting for you now in the hut we've put aside for you.'

'Thanks be to God,' said Sister Mary simply. 'He was watching over us all the time, you know, Sam. And most of the people around here are good Catholics

272

— just as you are.'

Thomas stared at the ground, feigning an interest in a scorpion moving lazily in the dust. He had been afraid of this. Trust Sister Mary to bring it up. She was staring at him now, her eyes cool and appraising.

'You are still a good Catholic, I hope?' she asked.

Thomas muttered something. Sister Mary was shrewd. She knew something was wrong and she was going to find out all about it, there was no doubt about that. She had always been a figure of power in the area.

'Are any of the mission fathers left on Renbanga?' she asked.

'No, they've all been taken off. You're the only one left.'

'The only one?'

'The only European, I mean.'

Sister Mary looked as if she were going to protest, but changed her mind. She had always been quick to strike if anyone tried to establish a difference between Europeans and Melanesians, Thomas remembered.

'Now tell me about Manno, if you please,' she said.

As they sat sheltered from the morning sun Thomas told Sister Mary Maria the story of McKinley and his transformation into Manno. His account was stumbling and uncertain at first but gradually he gained in fluency. He left nothing out. When he had finished Sister Mary shook her head incredulously.

'I have never heard anything like it,' she said. 'I can understand the people being bewildered, but to hear that you and Mr Jessop and Mr Bannion have been condoning such wickedness . . . Well, I'm shocked.'

'It's not as bad as all that — ' began Thomas sheepishly.

'Not as bad?' bridled Sister Mary. 'Have you forgotten the First Commandment?'

'The first . . . ?'

'Thou shalt have no other gods before me!' Sister Mary stood up. 'That's what your Manno has been doing with the people of this island, Sam Thomas. He has been setting himself up as a false god.

Now take me to him, please.'

'Sister,' said Thomas unhappily, 'you must be careful with Manno. He is not like other men I have met. He is bitter and unhappy. He would not give you the respect that is your due.'

'At this moment it is not respect that I am interested in.'

'Eat and rest first.'

'No, thank you.'

Defeated, Thomas led Sister Mary through the village to the clearing on the far side. Before they reached the open space they could hear the crackle of rifle fire. When the pair of them came out of the trees there were about fifty warriors assembled. Five of them were on their stomachs, firing at bamboo targets on the other side of the clearing. McKinley was standing apart from the others, watching the target practice. Thomas took Sister Mary across to him. The half-caste noticed that standing among the young warriors was Benny, the youth who had been flogged at Kukala. The boy had turned up hesitantly a few days ago. McKinley had raised no objection to his presence. The youth had attached himself unobtrusively to the fighting men. Thomas had wondered at McKinley allowing this but had put it down as just another of the American's unaccountable actions.

'Manno,' he said, 'this is Sister Mary Maria. Sister, this is Manno.'

'Good-morning, Mr McKinley,' said Sister Mary, taking in McKinley who was clad in his customary blue lap-lap and looking, apart from his absence of tattoo marks, like any other warrior. 'I believe I have you to thank for rescuing us from the bush.'

'Don't give it another thought,' said the negro indifferently. 'It was Sam's idea. He kept pestering me until I sent the guides. When you've rested up I'm sending you all down to Kukala with him. If the radio's still working he'll contact Tulagi and get them to send a submarine for you. If the set isn't working you'll have to wait a week or so until a canoe can get to Tulagi.'

'Thank you.'

'You're welcome,' nodded McKinley in

dismissal, and turned away to watch the firing.

'Mr McKinley,' said Sister Mary, not moving. 'Could I have a word with you?'

'I'm rather busy, Sister Mary.'

'It's very important, Mr McKinley.'

McKinley sighed. 'If you insist, Sister Mary.'

McKinley and the nun walked away from the clearing, followed by a troubled Thomas. They reached the village and entered the American's hut.

'Sit down, Sister,' said McKinley, offering her a wooden stool. He squatted on the floor while Thomas stood uneasily by the door.

'I'll have to ask you to be brief,' went on the negro. 'I've got a squad to train.'

'I'll be as quick as I can. Mr McKinley, what you are doing here is wrong and wicked. I must ask you to stop.'

'You what?' asked McKinley in amazement.

'You must give up this Manno nonsense. In fact I think it would be better if you left Renbanga altogether. Yes, I think that would be the solution. You must come to Kukala with us and wait for transport to Tulagi.'

'Lady,' said McKinley after a pause, 'you've got nerve, I'll grant you that. Now you listen to me. I've got a sweet operation going for me here. It'll take more than a screwy dame to louse it up.'

'I can only assume that you don't know what you are doing, Mr McKinley. You're causing untold harm here and undoing all the work of the missions. Why, some of the people think you're a Christ-like figure.'

'I know it. What do you think I've been working on?' The negro nodded at Thomas. 'There's my Simon Peter. And somewhere outside there's a kid who almost gave me away to the Japs once. I've brought him back on the strength because I reckoned I needed a Judas as well.'

Sister Mary was on her feet, her cheeks flaming. 'This is monstrous! You've deliberately played on the faith and the superstitions of simple people to further your own ends. I won't listen to such blasphemy.'

'Well, that's fine. Sam here will take you to your hut. We'll try and get you down to Kukala tomorrow.'

McKinley walked to the door and stepped out of the hut. The sun washed over him. He stood enjoying the warmth. In the space of a few weeks he had grown accustomed to the heat of the rays on his bare body. For a moment the thought of the obdurate woman in the hut gnawed at his mind. It was not important, he told himself; he could not allow it to be important. All that mattered was the task he had set himself.

He began to walk past the huts. There were no longer any women or children to be seen. They had been moved to another village together with the old men. Only the warriors remained. Of these there were the twenty who had made the attack and a further thirty who had survived the rigorous tests imposed upon them by McKinley and Thomas. These were the men who would form the nucleus of his force.

He could have had another five hundred had he needed them. Ever since the success of the raid young Melanesians had been flocking through the bush to join Manno. McKinley had turned most of them away. He had arms and ammunition for fifty. When these warriors had been trained he would be able to use them as section leaders. Then would be the time to send for the others.

In the meantime every Melanesian on Renbanga was acting as a scout or a spy. The Japanese camps were under constant surveillance and their patrols were being tracked wherever they went. Ever since the raid on the refuelling station the Japanese had been acting like angry hornets. Their patrols had been combing the coastal areas for the attacking party. So far no Japanese patrols had penetrated far into the bush; there were not enough men available for that. McKinley guessed that reinforcements might be arriving soon, which meant that he would have to make his big strike before fresh troops arrived.

The negro stopped and watched six warriors practising bayonet fighting on bamboo targets suspended from trees.

Their movements were clumsy but vigorous. McKinley was satisfied. He had taught warriors what little he knew about small-arms and close combat fighting and they had proved eager pupils. Allied to their knowledge of the island and their new found pride in their fighting ability he would soon be ready to send out the call for all the fighting men of Renbanga to join him in his crusade.

★ ★ ★

At two o'clock the following afternoon the old man came out of the bush with his story. He was weary and travel-stained and sweat was running in grimy tracks down his emaciated body. The first guards who challenged him thought at first that he was just another elderly bushman going walkaround before returning to his home to die, but the urgency of his halting pidgin made them listen to him. When they grasped the content of his message and realised its importance they hurried him to Thomas.

The half-caste was instructing four Melanesians in the intricacies of a captured Japanese machine-gun. He had laboriously stripped the weapon down and reassembled it, and was watching the warriors doing their best to dismantle it in their turn. When the old man was brought to him Thomas kept his eyes on the busy warriors as he listened to the bushman's tale. Gradually he lost interest in the machine-gun until all his attention was on the old man. When the latter had finished Thomas spoke to the guards, ordering them to feed and shelter the old man but not to allow him to leave the camp. Then he went in search of McKinley.

He found the American sitting in the shade of a tree with four of the warriors. These were the men who had distinguished themselves on the raid and had been marked down as potential leaders. All four were about to be sent on a scouting mission to the airstrip. McKinley was sketching a diagram in the dust with a stick and the scouts were bending over studying it.

'Manno,' said Thomas.

Unhurriedly McKinley went on with his instructions. He murmured a final word of encouragement to the four Melanesians and watched as they scrambled eagerly to their feet and loped off. Then he stood up and walked over to Thomas.

'Trouble?' he asked.

'An old man from Kwari,' answered the half-caste. 'He brings news of the coastwatchers.'

'What news?'

'Two of them have been killed by the Japanese.'

'The hell you say,' blurted out a startled McKinley. He recovered himself. 'Which two?'

'He says the young man escaped. That means Bannion and Wallace have been killed.'

'Well now, isn't that a thing,' said McKinley slowly. 'I call it a right shame. I wanted to kill that Bannion man myself. Now I'll never have the chance. It's too bad.'

The American walked away. Thomas

stared after him. 'What about Jessop?' he called.

'What about him?'

'The old man says he's in a bad way. He's trying to get back to Kukala but he keeps wandering off the path.'

'Is anyone helping him?'

'No, they're carrying out your orders.'

'Good,' said McKinley, still walking. 'Keep it like that.'

The sound of singing, women's voices, clear and beautiful, drifted across the village in a swirl of unexpected melody. Thomas raised his head like a fish rising to the surface of a pond. It was a hymn in language, one that took his mind back to another time in another place. He walked towards the hut that was the source of the noise.

Sister Mary Maria was standing in the cool gloom of the interior of the hut, conducting the six Melanesian sisters. Thomas stood at the back, listening. When the hymn had ended Sister Mary stared fearlessly at him over the heads of the other nuns, her back very straight.

'Good-afternoon, Mr Thomas,' she said

clearly. 'Have you come to take us to Kukala?'

'Not yet, Sister Mary. We start at sundown.' Thomas hesitated. 'I would like to stay and listen to the singing.'

'You are most welcome. We have already prayed for you and Mr McKinley. Sisters, *Jesus, lover of my soul.*'

For an hour Thomas stood against the wall of the hut. The voices rose and fell in intricate harmonies. The events of the past month rolled in procession through the half-caste's mind. He thought of Bannion; he had liked the Austalian, the man had been quick-tempered and knew how to look after his own interests, but he had been brave and generous, two qualities appreciated by Melanesians. Now he was dead, his body defiled and left to rot, another white man to die unremarked in the islands.

There were other matters to think about as well. Thomas stood immobile at the back of the hut as the sister sang. Finally he made up his mind. He waited until the nuns had finished a hymn and nodded to Sister Mary as he moved towards the door.

'We shall see you at sundown, Mr Thomas,' said Sister Mary composedly.

'Yes, Sister,' said Thomas. 'At sundown.'

16

With the sun still dipping above the most distant trees Thomas made his way between the huts to meet the sisters. They were already waiting for him under the large tree at the edge of the village. Somehow they had managed to clean their robes. They were all pointedly ignoring McKinley who was standing with two warriors outside one of the huts. The American nodded as Thomas approached.

'I'm sending Ezekiel and Welchman with you. When you get to Kukala try and contact Tulagi by radio if its still working. If not, send Ezekiel up by canoe. Whichever way it is you get back here as fast as you can. I'm going to need you soon.'

'Are you calling the men in from the villages?'

'That's right. I made up my mind this afternoon. Things are hotting up. We've got to move soon. I'm sending the messengers out tomorrow. I want every fighting man on Renbanga here by the middle of next week. We'll move in on the Japs on Saturday. So get the lead out.'

Thomas walked across to Sister Mary Maria. As he moved, outwardly stolid and phlegmatic, he was achingly aware of how little time was left.

'We're ready, Mr Thomas,' Sister Mary greeted him. She lowered her voice. 'And I'd like a word with you when it's convenient.'

Ezekiel took his place at the head of the procession while Welchman went to the rear. In single file they moved out of the village into the bush. At first the path was relatively wide and Thomas was able to move up next to Sister Mary for a few yards.

'There you are,' she said. 'Sam, I've had some rather disturbing news from Sister Teresa. She had heard that Mr Jessop, the young district officer, is lost in the bush. Is there any truth in this?'

'Yes, it's true.'

'And are you going to do something about it?'

'Yes,' said Thomas. 'I am.'

He looked around. They were well clear of the village and the jungle was pressing in on them. Already it was dusk and soon there would be no light at all. Neither Ezekiel nor Welchman would remark on his departure and both knew the way to Kukala. He raised a hand to Sister Mary and stepped off the path into the jungle.

'God go with you, Sam,' said Sister Mary.

* * *

There had been many people with him over the last few days, flitting in and out of his consciousness. Sometimes they merged into one another. Once his father had been there, rotund and cheerful. When he had spoken Jessop had leaned forward in order to hear him properly, only to discover that he was talking in the Are Are dialect. On another occasion an elderly bushman crossed his path and spoke to him briefly in Wallace's drawl. At

289

times the images became more distinct, as if he were waking from a nightmare to a reality only slightly less bizarre.

Always he tried to keep moving, placing one plodding foot in front of the other. Even when he had irretrievably lost the track he did not stop. The time came when he could no longer remember what he was running away from, but still he forced himself through the jungle. The steaming heat enveloped him suffocatingly and the branches and creepers raised cruel welts on his sun-blackened face and body. His shirt and shorts had been reduced to a few tattered shreds of cloth and he had abandoned his carbine and empty water-bottle.

Once he stopped to rest, crawling under a thicket in a futile attempt to escape the heat of the sun. He slept fitfully. When he woke up two Melanesians were staring curiously at him. Both men were carrying spears and had daubed war-paint inexpertly on their bodies. Jessop looked dully at them.

'Which way now?' he asked, speaking

through cracked and stiffened lips. 'Youfella lookem for killem finish?'

'No killem finish whitefella,' said one of the Melanesians indifferently. 'Manno speakim. Native no touchem whitefella. Spose whitefella die finish himi all right, but native no killem. Native go-go for killem Japani time bilong now.'

'Killem Japani?' croaked Jessop.

'True now. Manno speakim this time. Himi say all fella man bilong Renbanga himi go-go long Manno for fightem Japani close up. White man himi finish. Japani himi finish. Now man bilong Renbanga himi warrior all same time before. Manno speakem true.' The man raised his spear proudly. 'Renbanga bilong native man. Solomons bilong native man. Manno speakim true.'

With a grunted word to his companion the Melanesian stepped back. The two men hurried off into the trees and were soon out of sight. Jessop sank back into the undergrowth.

★ ★ ★

Thomas had slept for a few hours during the night but for most of the time he had been moving steadily through the bush. The old bushman had given him a rough idea of the route Jessop was taking and Thomas knew that Melanesians along the way would be observing the white man.

As he made his way along the half-obscured tracks he received ample confirmation of this. From women working in a garden he heard that Jessop was wandering blindly northwards. An old man gathering betel nut told him that the white man had crossed the main river of the island twelve hours before. Some youths gathering wood to build a hut confirmed that the district officer was in the area.

By the middle of the day Thomas knew that he was closing in on Jessop. He knew also that McKinley's messengers were fanning out over the island. Men, singly and in groups, began to pass him in increasing numbers on their way to join the warriors in the interior of the bush. They were of all ages and from many different villages, moving eagerly on their way to the high ground. Some of the older men were carrying fighting-sticks of great age, weapons that had been handed down the generations. It looked as if McKinley would be getting all the fighting men he needed.

Thomas discovered Jessop a few hours after noon, some twenty hours after he had left Sister Mary and her party. The Englishman was sprawled on his face among the undergrowth. Thomas hurried forward, afraid that he might be too late. Kneeling at the Englishman's side he turned him over gently. Thomas was shaken by the change in the district officer. Jessop was emaciated, his face burned almost black by the sun and covered with stubble. His breathing was shallow but regular.

Thomas straightened up, reassured. Jessop had been through a bad time but he was young and strong. Once he was taken to Kukala he should be able to recover in a few days. Thomas moved quickly away. There was a village in the vicinity. He would find two men there to help him carry Jessop.

They reached Kukala the following day and laid Jessop on a makeshift litter composed of branches. Bannion's former camp was overgrown with grass and creepers as the jungle reclaimed its own. Ezekiel and Welchman advanced incuriously and took over the stretcher. The two villagers melted back into the jungle. Thomas followed the stretcher to the largest hut. Sister Mary and some of her nuns hurried out. The Dutch sister went to Jessop's side and looked down with concern at him, feeling his pulse.

'Thank God you found him, Sam,' she said fervently. 'We'll take care of him now. There is food for you in Mr Bannion's hut.'

Thomas nodded his thanks and followed one of the sisters across to the hut once occupied by the Australian. The sister left him at the door and he went in. There were yams and pineapples on the table and a bamboo stick filled with water. Thomas fell hungrily on the food, it seemed a long time since he had last eaten. When he was satisfied he drained the water from the hollow tube and then sat down on a mat.

For a few minutes he allowed himself the luxury of feeling tired, sensing the weariness soaking into his bones. He stared round the room. This was where McKinley had fought Bannion that afternoon only a week or two ago. A great deal had happened since then. Accustomed as he was to the slow pace of island life Thomas found it difficult to believe that so much could have gone on in such a short period of time.

And in that time he had changed sides twice, Thomas reminded himself. Laboriously he tried to formulate the reasons for his actions, setting them out like a Bellona craftsman displaying his carvings on a mat. He had joined McKinley because he had been impressed by the confidence of the man and because he had thought the American, despite his motives, capable of uniting Renbanga for the first time in its history. He still believed this to be true but he knew that it was not enough. McKinley had been prepared to let Jessop die in the bush. It was true that men had to die in a war, but there was no mercy in the American. He was concerned only with killing those who had wronged him. He would raid the Japanese airstrip and kill many men and that would satisfy him. But what would happen afterwards? The Japanese would bring more soldiers to the island and kill every Melanesian they could find. McKinley would not care. Probably he would not mind if he was killed in the raid. There was nothing but hatred in him. He was not interested in the Solomons or its people. He was using them for his own ends, just as the foreigners had always done. There was nothing to chose between any of them.

Ten minutes later the door of the hut opened and Sister Mary came in to the room.

'I think he'll be all right,' she said. 'He's starved and the sun has treated him cruelly, but if he rests he should recover. Sam, I hate to nag you, but do you think you could see if that radio works?'

Thomas nodded and stood up. 'I'll look at it straight away,' he promised.

* * *

Jessop came round towards the end of the following day. Bannion allowed him time to eat and then went in to see the district officer. The Englishman was lying on a pile of mats against a wall. His smile when he saw the half-caste was more a grimace of pain.

'Hullo, Sam,' he said weakly. 'I hear we've been going walkaround together. Thanks. Do you think you could put me in the picture a bit?'

Thomas sat at Jessop's side and told him what had been happening over the last week. Jessop heard him out in silence, staring at the roof of the hut. When Thomas had finished it was some time before the Englishman spoke.

'It's all been one bloody great balls-up, hasn't it?' he said finally. 'Nothing's gone right. We've all blundered from one mess to another. We'd have done better if we'd never even started.'

'It's too late for that,' said Thomas bitterly. 'About fifty years too late.'

* * *

They had eaten their evening meal around a fire in the compound. Now the Melanesian nuns had gone to bed and only Jessop and Sister Mary were sitting by the embers. Thomas was in the radio hut, working on the transmitter. He had been there for most of the day. Sparks from the smouldering wood drifted into the air before sinking back like exhausted scarlet butterflies. The water of the creek slapped gently upon the shore. About them the jungle was a black mass against the night.

'It was the futility of it all,' Jessop was saying with a weary note of bewilderment in his voice. 'There was no reason for Bannion or Wallace to die. They both seemed to go mad.' He stared into the fire. 'I don't understand any of it.'

'We all have to do our best to understand, Mr Jessop. The Bible tells us that the man without understanding remains in the congregation of the dead.'

Jessop shook his head. He had shaved with Bannion's razor and was wearing shorts and a shirt which had belonged to the Australian. His face was drawn and haggard and he looked much older than his years. His movements were slow and uncertain and there was a new vulnerable air about him.

'I don't know anything,' he muttered. 'Anything.'

The door of the radio hut opened and Thomas stepped out. He walked across the clearing and squatted by the fire.

'I've got through to Tulagi,' he said. 'They're sending a submarine. It will be here at midnight on the 18th. That's three days away.'

'Three days?' Jessop rose. 'I'd better have a word with them myself.'

'You can't,' said Thomas, not looking up. 'I've smashed the set.'

'You've what?'

'I've smashed the radio. It's all right, I've arranged for you to be picked up. You've got nothing to worry about.'

'But why?' cried Jessop in amazement, advancing on the half-caste. 'What did you do it for?'

'I don't want any more contact with

people outside the island. This is a Renbanga affair. Nobody else is going to interfere.'

Thomas straightened up until he was towering over the Englishman. Sister Mary looked on unhappily but made no effort to interfere. Thomas was sullen and watchful, waiting for Jessop to make a move. The district officer controlled himself.

'I know it's an awkward situation,' he said. 'McKinley's got the entire island on his side. He's not a pleasant character. I don't like him any more than you do. But he's going to attack the airstrip. That's the important thing. He's the only man who can pull it off.'

'It means everything to you, doesn't it?' asked Thomas roughly. 'You want that strip destroyed.'

'Of course I do,' blazed Jessop. 'So far the whole thing's been a shambles. I'd like to salvage something from the wreckage. If that strip's destroyed it might make up for the rest.'

Sister Mary Maria stood up and wished the men a quiet good night, walking across to the hut she shared with the other nuns, her gown brushing against the ground as she went. Neither man paid any attention to her departure. The mood of both had turned to anger.

'That's all you care about,' said Thomas. 'The white man's war; that's the only thing that matters.'

'At the moment, yes. Once we've got rid of the Japanese we can begin to think of reconstruction.'

'Words,' said Thomas contemptuously. 'White man's words.'

'I don't understand you, Thomas. What are you going to do?'

'I'm going to do my best to stop a lot of islanders getting killed for nothing.'

'You'll never stop McKinley now. Nobody could. It's too late.'

'I can try.' Thomas began to extinguish the fire by kicking earth over it. 'Go back to Tulagi,' he advised. 'Leave Renbanga to the people who live here.'

'Oh no,' said Jessop. 'That submarine is for the sisters. I'm staying on the island. McKinley won't have me at any price but I want to be around to see what happens.'

'Haven't you had enough of the bush?' asked Thomas. 'You've almost died in it once already.'

'Then I'll have to risk dying in it again.'

Thomas opened his mouth to argue but changed his mind as a thought occurred to him. 'All right,' he shrugged. 'Come with me if you want to. I may need a white man — and I never thought I'd live to say that.'

17

There were five hundred men in the village, all between the ages of eighteen and thirty. Once there had been over a thousand but McKinley had sent all the youths and the men over thirty back to their villages. The ones who were left were sleeping in the huts and spilling over on to the ground outside. Each man had brought his own fighting-spear and a supply of sweet potato. The fifty warriors who had been trained by McKinley were now in charge of squads of ten.

It was anything but a well-balanced or properly equipped force, thought the American, but on their own ground and utilising the element of surprise these men were capable of destroying the Japanese airstrip. And after that? After that there would be a lot of dead Japanese.

McKinley raised his head and stared around the silent village. He was sitting under a tree on the edge of the camp. It was early afternoon. The warriors had eaten and, except for a few guards, were resting. In an hour they would resume their training. The following day was Friday. In the morning they would all move out. On Saturday they launched their attack.

Things had not gone badly, he decided. It was a pity about Thomas's defection but that could not be helped. The man had spent too much time with the whities; he was spoiled. The last that had been heard the half-caste had moved back into the bush with Jessop. They were welcome to it. Nobody was going to help them, that was for sure. All the same, it would be safer to take one basic precaution. McKinley beckoned one of the guards who was patrolling the village. The man hurried over to the American.

'Yes, Manno?' he enquired eagerly.

'You speakem long men bilong village,' McKinley ordered. 'Spose onefella himi see Thomas or himi see Jessop, mefella wannem twofella himi kill-kill finish, you savvy?'

* ★ ★

'I can't help you,' said Voli, fear seeping into his voice. 'Manno would kill me if he knew you were here.'

The fat headman was sweating. The perspiration rolled in great balls down his face. Jessop and Thomas sat opposite him in his hut. There were armed men outside the hut but Voli had ordered his guards to leave the hut as soon as he had realised what his visitors wanted.

'You shouldn't have come here,' he went on. 'There's nothing I can do for you.'

'You don't understand,' said Jessop patiently. 'As the representative of the Government I am ordering you as headman of this village to give me assistance.'

'Mr Jessop,' Voli begged piteously, 'please don't ask me to do this thing.'

'Of course,' added Jessop, 'I could always decide to investigate the matter of that Japanese patrol being brought back to this village the last time I was here. Naturally that would come under the heading of treason, which is punishable by death.'

'I could hand you over to Manno now,' blustered Voli uneasily.

'That would be extremely foolish. I sent a radio message to Tulagi before I left Kukala,' lied Jessop. 'I told the American general that I was going to the loyal Voli. If anything happens he will know that you betrayed me.'

'Anyway, why should you help Manno?' put in Thomas roughly. 'What has he done for you? I thought you were going to be one of his big men. Look at you! He won't even have you in his village.'

The headman scowled as the thrust went home. Jessop leaned forward. It looked as if Voli might be beginning to crack. It had taken them a hard night's walking to reach his village. Thomas had done his best to make sure that they had not been observed but it was impossible to tell how successful they had been. Voli had certainly been surprised when the pair of them had turned up that morning. It was a surprise which had swiftly turned to panic when the implications of their visit dawned on him.

'Why have you picked on me?' he demanded hysterically.

'Because you're a man who believes in looking after himself,' Thomas told him flatly. 'You want to please the Japanese, the English and Manno. All right, today you please the English.'

'What do you want me to do?' asked Voli, his voice sinking to a despairing whisper.

'We want to get to Manno without being seen,' said Jessop quickly. 'We want you to get us to him.'

Voli sat bolt upright. 'Impossible,' he gasped. 'It can't be done.'

'I want to follow McKinley when he makes his raid,' said Jessop. 'I don't care how I get there but I want to be on the spot so that somebody can report back to the Americans.'

'There is no way,' said Voli.

'Yes, there is,' said Thomas. 'That's why I have brought Mr Jessop to your village, Voli.'

'What do you mean?'

'I mean that McKinley will be coming

to the reef for the offering. We want to wait in the village until he comes.'

'What offering?' asked Jessop, annoyed and thrown off balance. 'You said nothing about any offering, Thomas.'

'Why else do you think I brought you with me? Did you think I was going on a bush walkaround like an old man ready to die? I brought you with me because I knew that you could persuade Voli with your threats of the Americans. McKinley will be visiting the reef off this village before he takes his men on the attack. It's one of the fighting customs of Renbanga, and the old men will have told him of it. Before a small raid the leader must sacrifice to the eagle, the fighting bird. Before a battle he must also sacrifice to the shark, the fighting fish. That sacrifice has to be made from a reef. The reef off Voli's village is the biggest in these parts.' Thomas returned his attention to the headman. 'When does Manno come here?'

'Tomorrow morning, an hour after sunrise.'

'How many men will be with him?'

'I don't know. Not many, just a small party of his leaders, I think.'

'That settles it,' said Jessop, recovering his composure. 'If we can't get through to McKinley's village we'll have to wait here for him.'

'That's what I was thinking,' said Thomas innocently.

'No!' cried Voli. 'Mr Jessop, I cannot allow — '

'Voli,' said Jessop, 'if you don't help us now I give you my solemn promise that when this war is over I shall return to Renbanga and personally see to it that you are hanged as a traitor.'

The headman gnawed one of his knuckles nervously, his eyes glazed with indecision. An unwieldy silence was broken only by the buzzing of flies. Finally Voli nodded his head unwillingly.

'You can stay in my village tonight,' he conceded grudgingly. 'No one will betray you. Tomorrow, before Manno arrives, you must both go out into the bush. What you do there is your own affair. If you are caught we shall say that we know nothing about you.'

'If we're caught,' said Jessop drily, 'it won't matter overmuch what anyone says.'

★   ★   ★

Voli allowed them to use the same hut that had sheltered Jessop on his last visit to the village. The district officer wondered if this could be an act of deliberate irony on the part of the headman, but decided against it. This was the guest hut, any strangers would be accommodated here. He sat on a pile of sacking and looked round the dusty room. This was where it had all started. He and McKinley had rested here and Senda had first had the idea of passing the American off as Manno.

'Do you think Voli will give us away?' he asked Thomas.

The half-caste shook his head. 'I doubt it. You frightened him with that talk of radio messages to the Americans. We should be safe enough if we don't wander too far from the hut until the morning.'

'And then what?' asked Jessop. It was a

question to which he thought he already knew the answer and had known it for some time. 'You said when we left Kukala that you wanted a white man with you. Why?'

'As a witness, of course,' answered Thomas. 'Tomorrow I'm going to kill Manno.'

★　★　★

Soon after dawn McKinley came down the ridge towards Voli's village. There were six warriors with him, all of them leaders he had marked out to play an important part in the forthcoming raid. The path was matted and overgrown. One of the Melanesians was walking ahead, clearing a way for the others. McKinley watched the man's bush knife rise and fall and thought of the exhibition the previous evening.

The warriors had gathered in the square and there had been the songs and dances of war. The men had moved like fluid shadows in the light of a large fire which sent its flames roaring into the air.

311

One Melanesian had performed the bush knife dance, whirling the implement about his head and body in incredible flashing arcs. It had been a fascinating exhibition of control and dexterity. A leader had informed McKinley that it was an art handed down from father to son since the days of the slave labour on the Queensland sugar plantations. At night, after a day's work in the fields, the exiled Solomon Islanders had perfected this knife dance. Some of them had brought it back to the islands and it was still being performed by their great-grandchildren fifty years later.

McKinley squinted up at the rising sun. One of the leaders had told him that it would take an hour to reach the reef. He deplored the time it would waste but he realised how much importance the Melanesians placed in their customs and traditions. The warriors would not move off that afternoon until they had heard from their leaders that Manno had made his sacrifice to the sharks. Once he had accomplished this they would follow him wherever he led.

★ ★ ★

'It's an hour after sunrise,' said Thomas. 'They should be here soon.'

He and Jessop were standing among the trees just outside Voli's village. The headman had hustled them from their hut at dawn and made sure that they were well clear of his village. From where the pair of them were hiding they could see the white sand leading down to the water's edge. The reef was about half a mile out. The waves seethed over the line of rocks before making the final approach to the beach.

'A man can stand on that reef if he's agile enough,' commented Thomas. 'They'll row McKinley out there and leave him to make the sacrifice alone. I'll be out there waiting for him.'

'It's crazy!' burst out Jessop. 'What's the point of it?'

'Without a leader the warriors will go home. The Renbanga men will never serve under another Solomon Islander. If McKinley dies a lot of Renbanga men will live. This isn't our war. You and the

313

Japanese can kill each other if you want to. Just leave us out of it.'

'If you kill McKinley his warriors will kill you,' said Jessop.

Thomas did not answer at first. He was staring out to sea. 'It's time I left now,' he said. 'I want you to watch what happens. If you're lucky you'll get back to Kukala in time to get on the submarine the Americans are sending for Sister Mary. If you get back to Guadalcanal tell the Americans and the British that we don't want their war on Renbanga.'

'They'll see you swimming out,' said Jessop desperately.

'Voli won't give me away, not at first anyway. He'll wait and see what happens and he'll tell his people to do the same.'

Thomas moved away through the trees. A few minutes later he reappeared on the beach. He ran down to the sea and plunged in. He struck out steadily for the reef. The half-caste was a powerful swimmer but it took him some time to cover the half mile. Eventually he hauled himself up on the rocks and walked quickly along the reef, the waves crashing over this body. Then he lowered himself back into the sea on the far side of the rocks. He would be clinging to the reef, judged Jessop, but even a man of Thomas's strength could only stand the buffeting against the rocks for a limited period.

A quarter of an hour later McKinley appeared on the shore. He walked down the beach from the village accompanied by Voli and six young Melanesians. None of the villagers had appeared. Presumably they had been ordered to remain in their huts during the ceremony. One of the warriors was leading a small pig by twisted coconut fibres. Two of the men ran ahead and pushed a canoe into the sea, holding it steady while McKinley and the man with the pig scrambled aboard. The two Melanesians pushed the canoe out a little further and then climbed in themselves and picked up paddles. Unhurriedly they headed for the reef.

After what seemed to the watching Jessop an interminable period the canoe reached the rocks. It floated a few yards off the reef, rocking in the heavy swell.

One of the Melanesians bent forward, securing a length of creeper to one of the seats. While the others paddled in unison to keep the canoe off the rocks the man leapt into the water, clutching the other end of the creeper in his hand. With a few economical strokes he reached the reef and hauled himself up on to the rocks. He turned and pulled at the creeper, playing the canoe towards the reef like a gigantic fish on the end of a line. The craft approached the rocks. McKinley stood up and jumped for the rocks. He landed awkwardly but retained his balance and stood upright, the water about his calves. The two men remaining in the canoe passed the pig over to him. The animal must have been drugged almost to insensibility because it hardly moved.

The negro was obviously having difficulty in keeping his balance, especially with the dead weight of the small pig under his arm. He looked on as the Melanesian on the reef discarded his creeper and dived back into the water. The others pulled the men back into the canoe and then began to paddle for the shore, leaving McKinley a solitary figure on the reef.

Jessop continued to watch from the shore, waiting for Thomas to appear. The half-caste must have known that the custom decreed that McKinley should be left alone to carry out his sacrifice to the sharks. At the moment the canoe was a quarter of the way back to the shore. The small group on the beach regarded the figure on the reef fixedly. McKinley drew a hunting-knife from the belt at his waist and held it high above his head. Then, still holding the pig under one arm, he swept the hand containing the knife down with a flourish, slashing the beast's throat.

Even from the shore the blood could be seen spurting out like a geyser. The pig squealed and kicked spasmodically. Methodically McKinley replaced his knife. Shifting his grip so that the pig was now clutched in both hands he shuffled forward and suddenly jerked the carcase forward into the water. He stepped back and bent down to wash his hands ostentatiously in the sea. It was then that Thomas appeared.

The half-caste was climbing over the rocks at the far side of the reef. The waves smashed over him, causing him to stagger from side to side but not impeding his progress to any greater extent. The American caught sight of the big man and swung round in amazement to face him. For a moment it was apparent that McKinley did not know what Thomas was going to do, but a snarled word from the giant sent the negro reaching for the knife at his belt. Before he could draw it clear Thomas hurled himself across the intervening space and dragged the American down to the reef.

The two men threshed furiously in the water, waves breaking over them and threatening to sweep them away. At first McKinley fought furiously, his knees thudding into Thomas's groin and his hands reaching for the big man's throat. Slowly, however, the half-caste's superior weight and strength began to tell. McKinley's efforts grew weaker and more disjointed. Soon he was lying inert beneath the other man. With throbbing strength Thomas held McKinley's head beneath the water. The waves thundered over them both but the half-caste did not relinquish his grip. After a minute McKinley ceased to struggle altogether. Thomas maintained his position for another thirty seconds and then rose, his chest heaving. He stooped and heaved McKinley's body out of the water. The muscles on his arms and upper body swelling he raised the corpse above his head and flung it into the sea, just as McKinley had earlier disposed of the carcase of the pig.

The canoe which had landed McKinley on the reef had been paddling frantically back as soon as the warriors aboard had seen Thomas appear. Now it reached the rocks and the men threw themselves over the side on to the lower slopes of the reef. Thomas met the first with a crushing blow to the head which sent the warrior toppling back into the water, but the second threw himself about the half-caste's legs while the third and fourth attacked with their hunting-knives from either side. Blow after blow descended on Thomas from the red-stained blades. He slithered down to the rocks. The warriors, possessed by grief and fury, hurled themselves across his body, continuing to drive their knives into his flesh.

Jessop turned away. No man could have lived through that onslaught. Now he has seen all the strangers on Renbanga except himself killed. Footsteps were coming through the trees towards him but he make no effort to escape. Voli appeared, stumbling towards him, sweating from the unaccustomed exercise. Jessop had not seen the headman leave the group on the beach. He wondered without emotion if Voli had come to gather credit by killing the district officer. Then he saw that the headman was alone and carrying no weapon. Instead he had stopped a few yards away, trying to recover enough breath to speak.

'Come,' he said finally. 'I will guide you back to Kukala. Manno is dead. It is finished.'

18

They carried the body of Manno reverently back up the ridge, singing the death chant of the gods as they went. One of the men climbed ahead and took the news to the warriors waiting at the camp. At first they would not believe the messenger and some of the warriors laid hands on him and beat him, but others went down the ridge to see for themselves. They met the party coming up the slope and helped carry Manno back to the bush village. Then they sent for women and told them to prepare the body according to custom. While this was being done the men cut down many trees and bushes and made a great pile in the clearing where the warriors had practised their fighting arts. This occupied the morning and the afternoon. When the sun went down at night the men who had accompanied Manno to the reef picked up his body and placed it in the centre of the pile of trees. Blazing torches were thrown on to the wood and all the warriors stood and watched in silence as the body of Manno was burned. Then, towards the early light of morning when it was all over, the men turned and walked away and began to journey back to their villages for now they had no leader to bind them together and lead them to glory.

★   ★   ★

'The whole thing's been a pig's breakfast from beginning to end,' declared General Kovacs. 'Nothing's gone right. Jessop, you're not free from blame not by a hell of long sight.'

Jessop did not answer. The commander in British Naval Intelligence who was the only other occupant of the general's tent also maintained a discreet silence. From outside came the bark of commands and the sound of marching feet. Jessop paid little attention to what was going on. He had been back at the American base on Guadalcanal for twelve hours. Two days before Voli had guided him safely back to Kukala and the submarine had picked up Jessop together with Sister Mary Maria and the Melanesian nuns at night and brought them safely to Tulgali. Jessop had then been interrogated by American and Australian officials before being flown to Guadalcanal at General Kovac's instructions. From the beginning of the interview the American had been in a black mood.

'Seems to me all you've done is watch other guys get killed and then hightail it away,' the general went on truculently. 'Now they're all dead. Wallace, Bannion, Thomas, McKinley, they've all gone. And you're alive, Jessop. I'd say that wasn't too much to be proud of.'

The intelligence officer cleared his throat apologetically. 'If I may say so, sir, you're not being altogether fair to Jessop,' he demurred gently. 'I'm sure that under the circumstances he did all that he could.'

'Fair!' Kovacs went almost purple as he glared at both Englishmen. 'I'm not here to be fair! I'm trying to fight a war. I wanted that airstrip put out of action. I was relying on it. You sure as hell failed, Jessop. I'm telling you here and now it's lucky for you you're a Limey. If you'd been under my direct command you'd be on your way to the stockade for dereliction of duty. Why the hell didn't you string along with McKinley and let him carry out that raid? I don't give a damn what his motives were; if he'd smashed the strip he would have done us all a favour.' He glanced at the commander. 'No chance of that private army of his carrying out the raid on its own account, I suppose?'

'I'm afraid not, sir. We picked up two Renbanga fishermen last night. They say that the warriors gave McKinley a traditional funeral and then dispersed. They dislike each other too much to join together without a leader they'll all accept. I'm afraid we'll get little co-operation from Renbanga for the rest of this war.'

'What about the headman who helped Jessop?'

'Voli? Our records say he's just an

opportunist. He guided Jessop to safety in order to store up credit with the authorities after the war. He'd never get the Renbangas to follow him in a crusade the way Manno almost did.'

'Manno!' General Kovacs shook his cropped head in disbelief. 'That man was just a big buck nigger from New York. How the hell did he end up as a god?'

'He was needed,' said Jessop, speaking for the first time.

'I don't know what that means and I don't care,' snapped General Kovacs. 'I might as well tell you right now that you're being re-allocated to Australia. I daresay they'll find somewhere to hide you for the rest of the war.'

At a sign from the commander Jessop stood up and turned to leave the tent but a curt word from Kovacs restrained him.

'Another thing,' said the American. 'Why did Thomas act the way he did?'

'He felt that it was his duty,' answered Jessop. 'As a half-caste he was never really accepted by the Renbanga people, yet he loved the islands. You don't have to be born in a place to be a patriot. Thomas

325

knew that what McKinley wanted to do was wrong for Renbanga and the Solomons.'

'And I suppose you do as well?'

'Now that I've thought about it, yes.'

'Mad,' said Kovacs wearily. 'I think every white man on that island went mad and that Thomas and McKinley followed suit. All right, get out and don't ever let me see you again.'

Jessop walked out of the headquarters tent. He felt no regret or remorse at Kovac's words. He was detached, oddly removed from feeling. It was as if everything had happened to someone else. The bustle of the camp surrounded him as he walked between the tents and huts. Squads of soldiers were being drilled in the sun, while orderlies and clerks hurried past. Ships were being unloaded in the bay and at the quayside sweating Melanesian labourers were stacking crates on to trucks.

'Chris,' said a voice. 'How are you, my boy?'

Jessop looked up to see Father Tulloch regarding him anxiously. As usual the priest was wearing baggy grey flannels and a creased floral shirt. There was an expression of concern on his face.

'Father,' said Jessop. 'I thought you were going walkaround across the island.'

'I've been to the weather coast and back,' said the priest. 'There was less to do than I feared. But how are you? Sister Mary Maria told me all about what happened. I'm very sorry about Wallace and Bannion and the others. In their ways each of them cared for the islands.'

'Yes, I suppose they did,' said Jessop.

'That's important, you know,' said Father Tulloch, his eyes fixed on the district officer. 'Every man must have a thing to love. Sometimes its a person, sometimes it's a place. A love for the islands is a thing that's bound a lot of very different people together over the last hundred years.'

'A hundred years is a long time,' said Jessop.

'In God's scheme of things it's less than nothing,' said Father Tulloch. A quick smile illuminated his face beautifully. 'You may have met my colleague

Father Schmeling on San Cristobal. He's ninety-three years old, you know. We were talking of bishops once and Father Schmeling said 'Bishops. *Just the fluttering of butterfly wings! I've seen six come and go in my time.*' ' The priest was serious again. 'You're one of those men who love the Solomons, Chris. I've been made aware of that in the short time you've been here. I hope that nothing has happened to diminish that love, because through it you're serving God.'

'I've been sent away,' said Jessop. 'They're sending me to Australia.'

'I see,' said the priest gravely. 'That's bad news. But the war will end one day. You'll be back, and you'll be needed. The islands will be a different place then. The war will have seen to that. So will the sacrifice of men like Sam Thomas. You've been through a bad time, Chris, and because you're young you'll probably blame yourself for things that weren't your fault. But this has been an apprenticeship for you. You've learned things — about yourself, about other people and about the islands. We'll need

328

that knowledge and that experience when the time comes to build the Solomons again. You do want to come back, don't you?'

Jessop looked about him beyond the shambles of the base camp. The sun was shining on the blue sea and canoes were dappled like pendants across the bay. On the beach a few palm trees not cut down by the Americans were shivering delicately in a soft breeze.

'Yes,' he said. 'I want to come back.'

THE END

We do hope that you have enjoyed reading this large print book.

Did you know that all of our titles are available for purchase?

We publish a wide range of high quality large print books including:
Romances, Mysteries, Classics
General Fiction
Non Fiction and Westerns

Special interest titles available in large print are:
The Little Oxford Dictionary
Music Book, Song Book
Hymn Book, Service Book

Also available from us courtesy of Oxford University Press:
Young Readers' Dictionary
(large print edition)
Young Readers' Thesaurus
(large print edition)

For further information or a free brochure, please contact us at:
Ulverscroft Large Print Books Ltd.,
The Green, Bradgate Road, Anstey,
Leicester, LE7 7FU, England.
Tel: (00 44) 0116 236 4325
Fax: (00 44) 0116 234 0205

THAT INFERNAL TRIANGLE

Mark Ashton

An aeroplane goes down in the notorious Bermuda Triangle and on board is an Englishman recently heavily insured. The suspicious insurance company calls in Dan Felsen, former RAF pilot turned private investigator. Dan soon runs into trouble, which makes him suspect the infernal triangle is being used as a front for a much more sinister reason for the disappearance. His search for clues leads him to the Bahamas, the Caribbean and into a hurricane before he resolves the mystery.

THE GUILTY WITNESSES

John Newton Chance

Jonathan Blake had become involved in finding out just who had stolen a precious statuette. A gang of amateurs had so clever a plot that they had attracted the attention of a group of international spies, who habitually used amateurs as guide dogs to secret places of treasure and other things. Then, of course, the amateurs were disposed of. Jonathan Blake found himself being shot at because the guide dogs had lost their way . . .

THIS SIDE OF HELL

Robert Charles

Corporal David Canning buried his best friend below the burning African sand. Then he was alone, with a bullet-sprayed ambulance containing five seriously injured men and one hysterical nurse in his care. He faced heat, dust, thirst and hunger; and somewhere in the area roamed almost two hundred blood-crazed tribesmen led by a white mercenary with his own desperate reasons for catching up with the sole survivors of the massacre. But Canning vowed that he would win through to safety.

HEAVY IRON

Basil Copper

In this action-packed adventure, Mike Faraday, the laconic L.A. private investigator, stumbles by accident into one of his most bizarre and lethal cases when he is asked to collect a fifty thousand dollar debt by wealthy club owner, Manny Richter. Instead, Mike becomes involved in a murderous web of death, crime and corruption until the solution is revealed in the most unexpected manner.

ICE IN THE SUN

Douglas Enefer

It seemed like the simplest of assignments when the Princess Petra di Maurentis flew into London from her island in the sun — but anything private eye Dale Shand takes on invariably turns out to be vastly different from what it seems. Like the alluring Princess herself, whose only character flaw is a tendency to steal anything not actually nailed to the floor. Dale is in it deep, mixed-up with the most colourful bunch of fakes even he has ever run up against . . .

THE DRUGS FARM

P. A. Foxall

The police suspect an American hard-line drugs dealer escaped from custody to be in England and they know of the expensively organised release from a maximum security prison of an industrial chemist. Their investigations are hampered by their sheer innocence of the criminals' resources and capacity for corruption, even in the citadel of power. No wonder there seems little chance of uncovering the criminals' product — a dangerous and hallucinogenic drug — that could threaten the young everywhere.